W9-DHF-566

THE SIGN OF THE
PRAYING TIGER

Books by Ben Lucien Burman

BEN LUCIEN BURMAN

THE SIGN OF THE
PRAYING TIGER

DRAWINGS BY ALICE CADDY

 The New American Library

Copyright © 1966 by Ben Lucien Burman
Illustrations Copyright © 1966 by Alice Caddy

All rights reserved. No part of this book may be reproduced without
the permission of the publishers.

First Printing

Published by The New American Library, Inc.
1301 Avenue of the Americas, New York, New York 10019

Published simultaneously in Canada
by General Publishing Company Limited

Library of Congress Catalog Card Number: 66-17727

Printed in the United States of America

For Mildred Smith

Chapter I

I guess I better call the place Menang. Course that ain't the real name. But I don't want to start any more trouble. I had enough terrible trouble while I was there to last me the rest of my life. And I sure ain't wanting to have one of them Menang fellows coming after me with one of them twisted knives they call a kris. Or meet up some dark night with one of the fellows that ride the green bicycles and belong to that society they call the Harmonious Daggers.

I'll try to tell this as good as I can. I ain't been to school much, coming from way back in the Kentucky hills like I did, and I'm sure sorry. But I went down to Louisville once to sing a hillbilly song on what they call the radio Amateur Hour, and I've read just about every comic book there is, so maybe I ain't all dumb. There's a lot of education in comic books if you read them right, particular what they call the Great History comics, tell all about Alexander, and Julius Caesar, and Napoleon, and comics like that.

I think about what happened in Menang plenty. You wouldn't figure things would have gone the way they did, specially since we were just trying to help everybody. People are sure funny.

I guess I always wanted to travel. It was a pretty little place, Muleshoe, where I was born. We lived in a little cabin, with the mountains rolling off to the sky everywhere you looked, and the pine trees all around, smelling like the time my sister won a bottle of perfume in a contest spelling the names of the Presidents, and broke it the first day it come. But I always felt kind of shut in and wanted to see what was on the other side of the hills.

Almost ever since I was born I liked to think about things, how people get to be the way they are, and everybody's so different, even twin brothers. And how when you're lucky and well off the way pretty near everybody is in America, maybe it's your duty to help the other people around the world ain't had much chance, and help to get them to be like Americans.

Travelers were always staying at our cabin, because there wasn't any hotel. Plenty of times it was a Baptist or Methodist or Holy Roller missionary, riding through on horseback or a jeep, and they'd tell me stories about Japan and China and how the people there stood upside down all day praying and things like that. And I'd think I wanted to be a missionary, too. But I guess I ain't much for church going so I figured I wouldn't be so good. Sometimes it was a teacher going to run a school up the creek and I'd have liked to do that better than anything in the world, because I sure liked school, though I had to quit after I'd just been going a little while. People that been to school and college all their lives ain't got no idea what education means to people way back

2

there in the hills. It was sure a awful day when I found out I had to stop.

Pa worked in the coal mine at Muleshoe and when I was about twelve years old he give me a big dictionary his father give him, and I started reading it right through. I got as far as *krait*, that's a kind of snake, when the roof of the mine caved in, and Pa was pretty near killed. He was crippled awful bad, and turned out the mine hadn't got the right insurance or something, and he didn't get any money. So I had to stop school and take his place in the mine, because I had a couple of kid sisters to take care of besides him—Ma had been dead a couple of years. I was only fourteen, and course it was against the law, but I was pretty near as big as I am now, tall and skinny like a cornstalk the way it is with most mountain boys, and I looked like I was eighteen.

We were terrible poor, and Pa kept getting worse and needing more and more money for medicine, and my sisters needed a lot of things the way girls do, so I worked overtime as much as I could and didn't get much more reading done in that dictionary, only as far as *multi*—that means many. Someday I'm going back there and finish reading it. Ain't such easy reading as the comics, but it's nice. My oldest sister's got the dictionary now, but she don't appreciate it at all. She's living in Lexington, married to a fellow runs a fruit and vegetable business, and she's just interested in parties and things. She lets the baby sit on it to raise him up high when he sits at the table. It kind of hurts me for her to have it, like for a wild savage in Africa to have a picture of George Washington, and maybe using it for practicing with his bows and arrows. She ain't the dictionary type.

It ain't too easy working in a coal mine and I come back one time covered with coal dust and all worn out, and there was a fellow had asked to stop for the night said he was a painter, was painting pictures to fit any frame for a dollar. He was a fine fellow, been everywhere, and he was such a

3

wonderful talker I forgot all about how tired I was, and I sat up till pretty near daylight listening to him tell about the places he'd been.

Before he started painting he'd gone around selling eyeglasses for a big company in Chicago, and he still had a few little books, *Eyeglasses around the World*, showing pictures of people wearing glasses in Egypt and China and everywhere. They cost ten cents for postage and handling, he said, but he gave me one free.

He stayed in the cabin three or four days, and I had a couple of empty frames and I got him to paint pictures of both my sisters because I could see Pa wanted them bad, and when somebody's old and crippled like that you got to give them everything they want if you can. The pictures of people cost a dollar fifty.

I found a third frame, kind of scratched up, but it was all right, and he painted a picture of my dog to fit it, and for that one he gave me a special price of seventy-five cents. Only thing was my dog had kind of green eyes and the fellow'd used up all of his green paint after he got one eye done and he painted the other one red, so the dog in the picture had one red and one green eye, like the Catahoula hog dogs I seen later down in Louisiana.

I looked at the pictures in the eyeglass book he gave me and decided right then if I ever got away from the mine I was going around the world and see all those people some way. I figured maybe I could do it becoming a salesman, but he said it looked to him I didn't have the salesman touch. He seen me showing one of the neighbor's kids how to make a kite, and I'd spoke to him how I'd like to be a teacher maybe, and he said looked to him I was the quiet, thinking type and that teaching or something like that'd be just right.

Well, once you start in one of them coal mines you generally always stay there the rest of your life. But then one

4

night Pa died awful peaceful in his sleep and pretty soon after that both my sisters got married, and then I was on my own, and I began figuring what I was going to do. I thought about what the fellow painting the pictures had said about being a teacher, and I talked to the new teacher that just came to the Muleshoe school from up North somewheres, but he kind of turned up his nose and said it wasn't like the old times in the hills—I couldn't teach unless I had what they call a diploma. And course I didn't have anything like that.

And then me and three other fellows that had sat around the general store in Muleshoe playing guitars and banjos and singing hillbilly songs seen how everybody was starting hillbilly orchestras, and we figured we'd start one, too. We named ourselves The Muleshoe Mountaineers, and that was the time we went down to Louisville and I sang the song on the radio Amateur Hour.

Some people that heard it said I was pretty near as good as them big fellows in New York, and that I ought to be a regular on the hillbilly singing program in Nashville, and I'd have liked that fine. So I went down there, and a big music fellow in a red and black checked shirt listened to me sing, and he said I'd hear from him. But I never did.

I was talking to the man who runs the post office at Muleshoe, thinking maybe the letter'd got lost. But he said no, he figured I didn't hear from the music fellow because I wasn't related to him. He said if you ain't related to them people you ain't got no more chance than a fat mouse at a cat picnic, the way they say.

Well, we couldn't make a living with the music somehow, and for a while I tried raising dogs. The way I figure that's about the finest thing on earth, a dog. I'll walk fifty miles to see a good dog moving picture—you know where a dog saves a baby in a fire, or a man's going to be hung for murder, and his dog finds the hat or something the real

5

murderer throwed away, and then finds where the real kill-
er's hiding, and saves his master, just when they're starting
to pull the rope.

But the dog raising didn't work, neither. I decided to
leave the mountains then and join the Army, and they sent
me down to Fort Polk, in Louisiana.

I tried a couple of jobs after I got out, working in a cotton
mill near Atlanta, and running a section gang laying track
on the L and N out of Chattanooga, but I wasn't satisfied
with any of them.

I guess if I hadn't met G.B. that night I'd have never
heard of Menang and nothing would have happened. I'd
hitchhiked from Chattanooga to Memphis, and was having
a cup of coffee in a wagon diner there, kind of trying to
think what I was going to do next, when G.B. come stroll-
ing in and took a seat by me. You knew the minute you saw
him that G.B. was somebody. He's a blue-eyed fellow,
about medium size, with his stomach a little bit fat. His
round face is a little fat, too, and shaved smooth as a baby,
and his red hair is pasted down slick as a whistle.

He's dressed sort of sporty with rich, kind of checked
pants and a fancy shirt that's all over little red race horses.
He's wearing a green tie with a enamel ace of diamonds for
a tie clip, and with ace of diamond cuff buttons to match.

He was the kind you call a card, never saying anything
that wasn't a joke, and always slapping everybody on the
back, and having something funny to say to them quick
as lightning.

I guess I was looking kind of worried, because first thing
he did when he seen me he whacks me on the back so hard I
pretty near hit the floor, and says, "Cheer up, Toots. Your
funeral ain't till tomorrow." And then he says, "A laugh a
day keeps the sheriff away." And everybody busts out laughing, and I laugh, too, and everything's fine.

Most of the people in the diner was his friends—he came

from Memphis—and pretty soon he was playing all kinds of tricks on them, and had them laughing like they'd die. You could see right away everybody was crazy about him. I guess he could have got himself elected President if he'd have worked at it. He was sure a wonderful fellow.

Well, we got to talking and it turned out him and me knew some of the same people in my Army outfit down in Louisiana, and even if he was older than me, in about five minutes we was real buddies, thick as a couple of pieces of fresh fly paper. He was managing a little filling station for a rich old lady in Memphis, and he said he was short-handed, and if I wanted to, he'd give me a job. So I took it.

The more I seen of G.B., the better I liked him. He'd knocked around plenty, being a hobo and a pitchman in a carnival and working for a undertaker burying Indians out in Oklahoma, and I don't know what else. He'd been in jail a couple of times. But it wasn't his fault. Once it was his wife that he was paying alimony to in Kansas City done it to him. Some way it looked like he'd married two women at once, though course he hadn't. They'd got the papers mixed up or something.

The other time it was a fellow he met in the Army. G.B. and this fellow bought a racehorse after they got out of the service, and they were losing the races all the time, and then all of a sudden they won a big one, and went to collect the prize money. And just that day the track had a saliva test and the judges said the horse was doped. But G.B. told me he never had a thing to do with it. He didn't know his partner was a crook. He said he'd cut his throat with a butcher razor before he'd do anything wrong. Like I said he was a wonderful fellow.

Well, I worked in the filling station about half a year, I guess. Memphis was a good town. They had all kinds of comic books. And all of a sudden G.B. begins looking worried, and then one night he starts closing up about nine o'clock instead of the way he generally done around eleven. I was wondering why, but I didn't say anything.

And then when pretty near all the lights were out, he turns to me, and speaks mighty quiet. "This is my last night, Oral," he says—that's my name, Oral—"I'm leaving in the morning."

I was sure shocked, because I'd figured on staying at the station a long while.

"What's the matter, G.B.?" I say. "Looks to me like the station's doing mighty good. Maybe you can wait a couple of months before you quit."

"I can't wait ten minutes," he says. "A fellow's played me a dirty trick again. If I'm here when the station opens up in the morning I'll be in jail the next ten years."

Well, seems like besides managing the filling station he'd met an old buddy worked with him once in a carnival, and this buddy invented a new kind of automobile wax that in five minutes made a old broken-down car look like it just came out of the factory. It was a wonderful wax, and G.B. and the carnival fellow got up a company, and sold stock to the old lady that owned the station and to all the people that come to buy gas. They sold plenty of the stock because it looked like it sure was worth a million, and then a couple of hours ago a friend of his came and told him the carnival fellow had skipped town, and G.B.'d better do the same. The friend said there was some kind of acid in the polish and after a month it ate off all the paint so it looked like the car'd been sandpapered, and then it began eating big holes in the metal all over, like they were cut out with a shears. Course it wasn't G.B.'s fault. He didn't know the carnival fellow'd do a thing like that.

G.B. said he figured he'd get a job as deckhand on one of the barge line boats running on the Mississippi that come into Memphis, and asked me if I wanted to go along. G.B.'d got to be kind of like a father to me, and it didn't take me more than two minutes to decide. Next morning we were both swabbing decks on one of the big towboats heading down toward New Orleans. We hit the big town, with the ocean boats in the harbor going everywhere, and we was having a couple of beers on Bourbon Street, when G.B. suddenly turns to me.

"This river business is all right," he says, running his fingers through his red hair, the way he does when he's thinking. "But it's kind of baby stuff. New Orleans is the jumping off place for hell or anywhere. How'd you like to go to China and India and Singapore and see all them deserts and jungles and places?"

Course nothing could have pleased me more.

"It'll be wonderful to see the world," I say. "And maybe we can help them poor people plenty the same time. Maybe teach 'em things they ought to know, or go out in the jungles and cure 'em when they're sick, and then they kind of make you a king, the way you see in the movies."

Well, we find a freighter down at the docks going out there right off, and quicker than a preacher can pick out a counterfeit nickel, we were swabbing decks again, sailing on the sea instead of on the river. It was fine traveling on the boat, specially at night with the moon shining as if it was solid gold, like the gold watch the governor of Kentucky wore when he came to Muleshoe once to open a new bridge, and the flying fish shooting past you like they were gold arrows. And then the moon would go down, and the stars would be shining over you, bigger than any stars you ever saw before, looking like silver baseballs somebody was going to bat down at you any minute.

And then the sun'd come up and you'd see the porpoises swimming toward the boat, and they'd take their places in front of you, just as if they were motorcycle police escorting somebody, the way I seen them do a big general the time I went down to Louisville to be on the Amateur Hour. And you wondered if the porpoises really were men that God got mad at and turned into fish, the way they say.

And then, before you could turn around hardly, we were in Singapore. It was full of Chinamen, millions of little fellows like the Chinaman had the laundry back in Muleshoe I used to see spitting on the shirts before he ironed them. They were all living together on streets so crowded a snake trying to twist his way through would have broke his back. Little pushcarts were everywhere, piled up with shrimp and pork and clothes and cheap watches and hardware and lizards and funny animals they were going to cook and make medicine out of, all mixed up with men on bicycles selling hot tea and soup, and the giant Chinese they call Manchus, carrying trunks and wardrobes and pretty near a house and lot on their backs. Story-tellers were sitting around reading newspapers out loud to the people, because most of them couldn't read or write; and there were all kinds of fortune tellers they call astrologers, old fellows looking like magicians way back, wearing tight black skull caps, would ask you when you were born, and then they'd tell you by the stars if you ought to marry a blonde or a brunette, or if you were going to get killed by a automobile or maybe shot by a policeman.

Everywhere people's washing was hanging on wires and ropes over the street like signal flags on a ship in the Navy. G.B. said there wasn't a Chinese in the world hadn't run a laundry sometime. After the Chinese most of the people were what they call Malays, little fellows looked like the Filipinos I seen waiting table in a restaurant in New Orleans when me and G.B. were there, and one of them thought G.B. was smiling at the blonde girl was the cashier, and come at him with a knife.

Besides the Chinese and the Malays there were a lot of Hindu women in long robes they call saris, and Hindu men wearing turbans and a white handkerchief for pants. Among

all them small Chinese and Malays a tall skinny mountain-
eer like me must have looked kind of like that fellow Gul-
liver in the story when he went among the Little People.

We were both crazy about Singapore. "This is the place
we been looking for," says G.B. "It's a big town, rolling in
money, and they're crazy about American things. All we
need is a good idea."

He was sure right. Everywhere they were putting up
American snack bars, and cafeterias, and places selling ice
cream sodas, and swimming pools, and American drug-
stores, and even what they call a American success and personality school. We passed the school one day when they
were having a big party or something, and there were so
many people going in it was like election day.

Well, we were in Singapore maybe a week, I guess, looking around for something to do, when G.B. met a German
fellow from Berlin had picked up a bunch of American
jukeboxes and pin ball machines. He told G.B. he'd been
selling them like hotcakes, and was making a pile, but he
had a offer of a big job with a German company in Hong
Kong, and he was having to get rid of them cheap. G.B.
sure wanted to buy them, because he figured they'd go fine,
but he was kind of short of money after the wax business in
Memphis, so I lent him what he needed. G.B. said it
couldn't miss, and that we'd make a fortune. We started
taking them around to the tea houses and coffee places and
dance halls run by the Chinamen. But in about a minute
we learned the truth. That German sure was a terrible liar.
We couldn't sell one.

We stayed in Singapore a couple of months, trying to figure out something to do, when all of a sudden I seen that
same worried look come in G.B.'s eyes he had in Memphis.
And next thing I knew just before supper he was piling his
clothes in a suitcase.

"I got to be moving again, Oral," he says. "If I ain't out

of here by daylight I'll be drinking with the fish down at the bottom of the harbor."

It sure gave me a shock because I liked Singapore.

"Is it woman trouble?" I say.

He nods his head it's so. "It's like Kansas City," he answers. "Only this time I been mixing my drinks. One of 'em's a Hindu girl, and the other's Chinese. The Hindu girl's family's a terror. . . . Please don't ask no more questions. It hurts to talk about it. Like your throat when you got laryngitis."

I watched him a couple of minutes, and then I began throwing some things in a suitcase, too.

"Where we going now?" I say.

His round face kind of lit up with a smile, because I guess he thought I wouldn't come with him. But I sure ain't the kind that lets a buddy down.

"There's a boat out of here in two hours for Menang," he says. "That's a island a couple of hundred miles south of here. Down near the middle of Indonesia. They're crazier about Americans there than they are even in Singapore. And I figure we can make a million easy. I got all the jukeboxes and the pin ball machines aboard. Don't forget to take your pistol. I hear it ain't a Sunday School."

We got down to the wharf where a scrubby little freighter was just about ready to pull up her gangplank.

A Australian sailor was standing there, come off a boat from Sydney in the next dock.

"You going to Menang, mate?" he says.

"That's right, buddy," I say. "You heading there too, maybe?"

He started exploding Australian cusswords like he'd swallowed a stick of lighted dynamite.

"I been there once," he says. "And you couldn't get me back if the whole bloody island was covered with gold and a thousand of them bloody beautiful girls they got there was sitting naked in gold chairs with their arms out begging me to stay. Anybody goes to Menang's got a hole in his head big enough to drive a bloody bulldozer through. And if he ain't got it when he goes there, he'll bloody have it when he leaves. Or I guess it'd be a hole in his chest. 'Cause it ain't easy to push one of them twisty wisty krisses into a bloody skull."

We went aboard and in a few minutes we was heading out to sea. She was a funny little ship with a Chinese crew and a funny little Chinese captain. For a night and a day and another night we run, and then a city showed up on a island ahead, looking like one of the set of Chinese plates a uncle of mine brought Ma back from the war in the Pacific, was all painted up with different Chinese scenes. Everywhere you looked you saw Chinese temples and pagodas and the Malay churches they call mosques. It looked about half the size of Louisville, I guess, the time I went down for the Amateur Hour.

Even before we touched the wharf a bunch of half-naked Malays looking like pirates jumped aboard, and climbing up the side of the ship, grabbed our bags and run off with them, I didn't know where.

"It's Menang," said G.B., and we walked down the gangplank.

And that's how it all began.

Chapter II

We went ashore to a funny little Chinese hotel right by the docks, and took a trishaw—that's a rickshaw run by a man pedalling like it was a bicycle—around the town.

It was a beautiful place, so pretty it was like you were dreaming and were afraid every minute something would wake you up. Coconut palms so tall you could hardly see the tops were standing all around the edge of the sea, with the water so blue it didn't look real; you'd think somebody had poured in thousands of barrels of blue Easter egg dye. Everywhere it was dotted with Malay canoes, painted all the colors of the rainbow, with the little Malays standing in the bow holding a spear twice as high as they were, catching fish. With their brown skins they looked like the statues you see on fancy clocks, made out of polished copper.

Around the harbor were hundreds of little Chinese boats they call sampans, with families of half a dozen kids maybe staying on them and never having a home on land all their lives; the boats were all tied together so you could walk from one to another for maybe a quarter of a mile. After the sampans were a lot of Chinese junks with big colored sails, all roped together the same way, and then a bunch of Chinese loveboats; and on some of the loveboats you could hear Chinese girls singing.

There was a river, too, coming down from the mountains you could see back of town, and where it flowed into the ocean there were a lot of little houses built on stilts way out over the water. On the far side of the river there were rice paddies, with men and women wearing funny Chinese hats and driving big water buffalo. Beyond the rice paddies there was nothing but jungle, full of tigers and elephants and snakes the farmers said after they'd eaten something were bigger around than a telephone pole.

The people were about the same as Singapore, the Chinese eating all the time with chopsticks in little teahouses, and the Hindus looking awful solemn and wearing nothing but the handkerchiefs, and the Malays carrying the krisses, and a few of them people they call Thais from Siam, the same as the funny cats. The Thais were smiling all the time like a photographer was taking their picture and had asked them to show their teeth.

The women on the island were the most beautiful I ever seen, specially the Malay ones wearing what they call sarongs and the Hindu girls with big mournful eyes, kind of like Jersey cows. Wherever you went beautiful birds were singing and mynah birds were whistling, imitating bugle calls and bells and every sound they'd ever heard. And what they call lyre birds flashed through the trees, had tails looked like you could play music on them, they were just like a harp. Nobody ever talked loud, or nobody was ever in a hurry. The way I said, it was just like a dream.

"This'll sure be a fine place for the jukeboxes and the machines," said G.B.

They had some automobiles in town but they cost a lot; so we hired a cart with a ox pulling it—that was the way everybody done—and went around the teahouses trying to sell or rent the machines. But it was like Singapore. Nobody would touch them. All the music there was little orchestras of fellows playing gongs; and somebody said maybe the gong players were stopping us. Anyway we were stuck with the boxes again.

"We got to do something pretty fast," said G.B. "Our money ain't going to last forever."

Another week passed and things was getting pretty terrible. G.B. was reading the Singapore paper, when all of a sudden he jumps up and gives me a slap on the back so hard I could feel it come through to my ribs pretty near.

"I got it, Oral," he says. "Look there!" and he points to something in the paper he's holding.

"I can't see anything but some advertisements," I answer.

He gets kind of irritated. "That's just it," he says. "This particular advertisement." And he points to a ad saying that because it was growing so fast, the success and personality school we seen in Singapore was going to open a branch in a new building just put up near the Raffles Hotel.

"I guess I'm pretty dumb," I say. "But I don't know what you're meaning."

He's pretty mad now. "This is something you ought to like," he says. "Especially you always wanting to be a teacher and helping these people and everything. We'll start a success school here in Menang. You can't help anybody more than making them a success, and we'll make a mint of money besides. I was a fool for not thinking of it before."

I'm kind of doubtful for a minute. "How do you figure people'll like it?" I ask.

"It can't miss," he answers. "If it's a big hit in Singapore it's got to be a hit in Menang, too. Everybody here's crazy about everything American except the jukeboxes, and there's a reason for that I ain't discovered yet. The people here are just coming out into the world, like a kid putting on his first pair of long pants; and we got to teach 'em how to be a success when they've got the pants on."

He walks up and down like lightning the way he always does when he's excited, chewing the end of a cigar they call a cheroot all the big rubber planters smoke in Singapore.

"Everybody wants to be a success and to be a leader," he says. "Even dogs and cats, and I'll bet even a mouse or a flea wants to squeak louder or jump farther than his buddies if you could figure out how to ask 'em. Besides these people want a education more than anything else, like your people back in the hills. You see the pictures in the magazines all the time of them foreigners coming to America to study. The colleges are fuller of 'em than a possum's full of ticks."

Well, it sure sounded fine to me, specially since it was a school, the way I'd always wanted. But I was still a little worried.

"How'll you get to know how to run it?" I ask.

"That ain't a problem," he answers. "I know already. I got a book I bought in the States tells all about how to do the success business, and I've studied it plenty. Yessir, we've sure hit it right this time. These are smart little people in Menang, smarter than us maybe. And when we show 'em American ways, ain't no telling how far they can go."

We started looking for a place right away. We went around the empty buildings in the town but didn't find anything we wanted, and then we seen there were a lot of big houseboats anchored along the harbor, and one of them, tied up to a wharf in front of a rubber warehouse, was for rent cheap. It looked kind of like a Mississippi steamboat except it was painted all red and gold and was all covered with fancy Chinese curlicues. It'd been a floating teahouse, like they got out there.

It still had a sign hanging over the gangplank with its name, *The Praying Tiger*, and a picture of a big tiger on his knees, looking like he was asking to be forgiven for some sin, maybe eating a man. And the same tiger was painted on both sides of the bow.

It was a nice boat, with the gold scraped off in only a few places, and it had a big room running all the way from the bow to the stern that'd do fine for the school. Besides that it had a fine kitchen, having been a restaurant, and some little rooms off to the side where G.B. and me and anybody else could sleep.

"A tiger's fine luck out here," says G.B., and I see him patting his little bit of a stomach the way he does when he's feeling good. "Let's take it."

We paid the rent to the little Chinaman that come with us, and were just stepping back on the wharf when all of a sudden a big row broke out in the rubber warehouse in front of where the boat was tied. A minute later a big black automobile went dashing down the road making donkeys and Chinamen with carts and everything jump out of the way. And behind the car a half dozen little Chinamen came riding green bicycles, pedaling like crazy.

Some Chinese and Malay people were standing there, and when they saw the automobiles and the bicycles they started running off, like they were trying to get away from the smallpox. And then some policemen raced up, and some Chinese clerks in black coats came busting out of the warehouse and began waving their arms like windmills and jabbering their heads off. But the police just looked at them with faces like dead turkeys, and shrugged their shoulders.

A big crowd gathered fast, but we couldn't find out what was going on till I seen a sawed-off little Cockney, named Bertie, all shrunk up like a jockey, had a bar he called the Four Elephants a block or so down the harbor. G.B. and me went there for a drink once in a while.

"It's these bloomin' Chinese secret societies started the row," says Bertie. "They run this bloomin' place like they allus do everywhere out here in the East where there's any Chinamen. You take two Chinamen and put 'em together and you got a secret society. You take four Chinamen and you got two secret societies and a war."

"That's bloody right, mate," says his bartender, a big, red-faced Australian named Alf that's got a head and body like a bull and a voice like a bull when he's roaring. "All they do is kidnap people and get protection money that makes the bloody gangsters in Sydney and the States look like Salvation Army girls. And the coppers works right with 'em, just like innocent little daisies all growin' on the same bloody stem."

"What they done this time?" says G.B.

"Nothing except kidnaping one of the richest fellows in Menang owns this bloomin' rubber warehouse and a couple of hundred others," says Bertie. "But you needn't worry. They ain't kidnaped or asked for the bloomin' protection money from anybody but Chinese." He stopped and looked at us kind of funny. "That is they ain't done it yet."

Well, we took over the boat next day, and course first thing we had to do was get some servants to clean it up. We talked to Bertie at the bar and he said he knowed a man that would do, a old Chinese they all called Mock Duck. So we hired him. And then a Malay fellow came along looking for work, said they called him Amok, and we gave him a job, too.

They were both fine fellows and they sure worked hard.

This Mock Duck was a little old man so dried up all the yellow had washed out of him; his skin was a kind of muddy gray had cracks in it deep as Grand Canyon. He was wearing black pajamas, like the working people, and was all covered with dust from cleaning up the boat; he looked kind of like a old raccoon that'd climbed into a attic and got into somebody's old clothes.

All Chinamen kind of sing when they talk, but Mock Duck's voice was way up high; it was so old and dried out, I guess, and he sang a regular tune. He sounded just like one of them comedians you see in the movies imitating opera singers. I wanted to laugh plenty of times, but of course I didn't. I didn't want to hurt his feelings.

Like I said he worked hard, but he was the most superstitious fellow I ever saw. He was always doing something to keep from having bad luck, buying good luck charms in the market or putting up mirrors around the place to scare off the devils. He said the devils couldn't stand looking at themselves in a glass, they got scared of their own faces. But the thing he worried most about was the Kitchen God, a funny fat little statue he had near the stove, that all Chinamen believe watches what goes on in the place where the god is staying, and goes off to Heaven each New Year's to tell how the people in the house are behaving. Course the people are always wanting the god to make a good report. So Mock Duck was always giving him bits of the best food we had, and smearing his lips with honey and things to keep him in good humor. The Chinese are sure funny that way with their gods. They treat them just like they were a person. The Chinese people are what they call Buddhists. That's near the end of the B's in the dictionary.

The other servant, Amok, was a skinny young fellow, with coal black eyes and hair, looked like one of the Filipinos in the restaurant at New Orleans. He had a big scar on his face running down from his left eye that made him seem like he was a terrible fellow, but when you looked at him close you could see his eyes was awful sad, like a dog that'd lost her pups and was always going around looking for them. When he talked he spoke so low and gentle you could hardly hear what he said. And he wore a little wraparound skirt made him almost look like a lady.

He was getting along fine when I happened to mention his name one day to Alf, the bartender at the Four Elephants.

"What did you say they call him?" asks Alf.

"Amok," I answer.

"Jesus, Joseph, and Mary!" roars Alf, and his ham of a hand pretty near drops the bottle of whisky he was pouring.

"What's the matter?" I say. "You got a heart attack?"

"It's your bloody Amok," he says. "He's worked for a couple of Englishmen that used to run rubber plantations here. He's a bloody Bugi, comes from the Celebes Islands, where all the men are still bloody pirates. But worse than that, they get mad at something when you ain't expecting it and run what they call amuck, and race around with a bloody kris trying to kill everybody they see. This one's done it a couple of times, though they always stopped him before he's killed anybody. The Englishmen gave him that bloody name so anybody'd know if he turned up."

I guess I went pale, and hurried on back to the boat. G.B. was away, but I found Amok and asked him if what Alf said was true.

He began to cry like a baby and the big scar under his eye got all shiny with tears; he dropped to his knees and kissed my feet. It made me feel awful.

"It is true, Tuan Oh-ral," he sobbed. That's what the natives called me, Oh-ral. I guess it sounds kind of Malay or Chinese, and Tuan, that means Mister. "But I have only done this twice. I love you very much, Tuan. And I promise I will not do it again. Or if I feel it coming upon me I will tell you, and you can tie me with ropes and chains until the fever passes from me. Do not make me go, Tuan."

And he cried even more, like his heart was going to break.

Course I couldn't let him go when he was carrying on that way. A woman crying is bad enough, but hearing a man cry, I don't know, just kind of tears you to pieces, like you was caught in a meat slicer. And I knew he had a nice little wife and a lot of kids and everything. And besides, if I fired him, he might go amuck right away. When G.B. came back, I didn't say anything about it, because G.B. would have got rid of him in a hurry. So he stayed. But I was kind of worried.

Well, the longer I was in Menang the happier I felt we were going to open the school, because those people there sure needed helping more than anybody in the world, I guess. They didn't know as much even as the hillbillies back in Muleshoe. They were worse ignorant than old Ace Jackson they called Cottonbeard, lived up the creek back of our cabin, would argue with you by the hour the earth was flat, and said we was all descended from people in Sodom and Gomorrah that had escaped the fire when God wasn't looking.

It was a big job getting the school ready, because they'd never had anything like that in Menang before. We got a lot of second-hand chairs and put them in the big room that took up most of the boat, and then we found a big desk a English fellow had on a rubber plantation and put that at one end, and it looked like a real school.

Mock Duck's daughter was coming to help him now, a Chinese girl maybe nineteen or twenty named Mu Lan, meaning Beautiful Orchid, and that's sure what she was, a beautiful flower. I'd never really seen a Chinese girl close before—the Chinese fellow that spit on the shirts in Muleshoe didn't have a wife or anything—and I guess there ain't nothing like them anywhere. She was a tiny thing, this Mu

Lan, didn't come up to my neck hardly, with the smallest hands and feet I ever seen. When she came to work she was wearing kind of black pajamas like her father, the way the Chinese girls do. But when she was dressed up she had a red silk jacket and red trousers, all trimmed with gold, like the boat. When she walked you could hardly see her feet moving; she kind of glided as if she was skating on ice. When you looked at her in the red jacket and trousers if she had a key in her back, you'd have swore she was a Chinese doll, running by clockwork.

Everything about her was awful soft and delicate. When she talked she kind of sang a song, too, like her father. But when you heard her it wasn't funny like him; it was like real music, kind of like the water in the little creek near our cabin back home where it ran over some rocks.

Every day she kept bringing something different to make the place look nice, a Chinese paper dragon that stuck out a black tongue when you squeezed it, or a Chinese lion with a bell around his neck and long whiskers that'd shake for ten minutes after you touched them. Or maybe she'd bring a little envelope wasn't as big as a package of needles, and say, "This is a present for you, Tuan."

And she'd fill up a pitcher with water and put it on a table, and then she'd open up the envelope and take out a little piece of paper that was inside. And she'd say, "Please turn your back, Tuan."

And I'd do like she said, and in a minute she'd tell me to turn around again, and I would and the pitcher would be so full of flowers it wasn't big enough to hold them; little roses and bleeding hearts and lilies of the valley and every kind of flower you could think of, all come from the little piece of paper.

And she'd clap her hands and laugh awful soft and low; so soft it wasn't a laugh really. It was more like the little tinkle of the ice in the creek back home when it first began breaking up in the spring.

None of the things she brought ever cost much because she and her father were real poor. But they were sure pretty.

And sometimes she'd take a fan and play a kind of a game, smiling and opening and shutting the fan, kind of the way you shuffle cards; and hiding her face behind it for a minute, and then taking the fan away.

And then she'd do a funny little bow, like I seen the Japanese do in the moving pictures, and then she'd fold up the fan and laugh like the ice tinkling again.

She was real cute.

Well, everything on the boat was in good shape, and we were going to pick a date for the opening when Mock Duck said before we did anything like that we ought to go to the Chinese temple with him and see if it was all right with the gods around Menang for us to start the school. If we didn't, he said, something terrible would happen. Course G.B. and me said it was foolishness, but he kept arguing so hard, and after all he was Chinese and we wasn't, and we wanted to get along with the people in Menang. So we thought we'd better do what he said.

We went off one morning, G.B. and Mock Duck and Mu Lan and me. It was the biggest temple in Menang, what they call a snake temple, like they got some places out there, with the altar full of little green snakes that were deadly poison, twisting and squirming, with the priests letting them wind around their arms, just like they were a bunch of rubber bands they'd bought in the dime store. It sure reminded me of the Holy Roller snake-preachers used to come around Muleshoe.

Some of the people were kneeling down, worshiping the snakes, and some of them were shaking bamboo holders full of little sticks and then throwing out a stick and looking at the number. I been in all kinds of churches, Baptist, and Methodist; and I went into a church near home once where there was some Catholics, and seen the priests ringing kind of sleigh bells and dipping holy water. But this was the funniest church I ever seen. It was more like playing Bingo.

Mock Duck took one of the bamboo holders hanging in a rack on the wall like billiard cues, and he begins shaking it like the others. And pretty soon one of the sticks falls out and he runs over with it to a priest sitting there; and the priest takes a holy box full of little ivory tablets with numbers on one side and writing on the back, and he picks the tablet with the same number that Mock Duck threw, and reads him what it says. And the big cracks in Mock Duck's skin sink deeper; his face looks like one of them hundred-year-old eggs they have there before you knock off the dried mud they're packed in.

He hurries over to us, and his high voice is shaking like he was freezing to death.

"The gods have spoken, O Tuans," he tells us. "They say you must not open the school."

We both tell him he's crazy.

"Go back and talk to the priest again," says G.B.

Mock Duck goes, like G.B. said. And the priest waves his arms, all excited, and a minute later Mock Duck comes hurrying back.

And this time his face is like it's covered with gray dust, like it's the egg with the mud just knocked off. "The priest says if you open the school something terrible will happen, O Tuans. One of you will die."

Course we weren't going to let a crazy thing like that stop us, and went right ahead with what we were doing. Though once in a while after that I'd wake up in the night hearing the gongs playing in the distance and somebody singing them queer Chinese or Malay songs; and all the things you'd seen in the picture shows come back to you, and you sure got to feeling pretty creepy.

Mock Duck went around awful gloomy now, looking like he was expecting something to happen any minute. And all the time he was praying before the Kitchen God and giving him more fancy things to eat. Mu Lan prayed before the god, too, but she wasn't scared of him as much as Mock Duck.

The more I saw of Mu Lan the cuter she got. And she could do all kinds of things. She was wonderful doing embroidery, and she could paint Chinese pictures, too. And whenever she had a minute you'd see her working with a needle, making some kind of fancy tablecloth or something for the boat, or painting a picture with lines so fine you could hardly see them, mountains, and fishermen, and deer, and tigers. I saw her draw a tiger one day, and she drew a couple of stripes on the tiger first, and then painted the rest of the tiger onto the tail. G.B. said the Chinese do everything backward.

Every day we worked hard, fixing up the school. We put up a big sign made out of cloth ran almost the length of the boat, *Menang Success School.* And then we studied the book G.B. had and put signs all over the big room, *Develop Your Hidden Personality, Knowledge Is Power,* and *Every Man A King.*

We left the sign with the praying tiger over the gangplank and we didn't paint out the tigers on the bow. Like G.B.'d said a tiger out there was good luck, and Mock Duck said a praying tiger was the best luck of all.

I was outside tacking down our big sign about the school that had got loose in the wind when there was a lot of excitement in the rubber warehouse where they'd kidnaped the rich Chinaman. First I saw some fellows riding green bicycles race past, just like the ones I saw before. And then a sports car drove up, and a rich-looking Chinaman stepped down from it, and all the Chinese clerks in loose black shirts and pants came running out, and shook his hand, all smiling.

"It is the rich man come back from the kidnapers, Tuan," said Mock Duck, shivering all over. "He returned to his house last night. They say he has paid them $50,000."

Well, like I told you I think a lot, and part of thinking is finding out things. In the back of the dictionary I had there was some pages, Wisdom of the World, and it said there when you stop wanting to find out things you might as well be dead. And I figure that's sure right. The only kind of secret societies I knew about before were the Masons and the Oddfellows and people like that, had parades and carried tin swords and wore aprons and funny hats. I started asking Mock Duck about the secret societies in Menang to see if he'd tell me any more than Bertie and Alf. At first he wouldn't talk. But when I kept asking, he looked around like a old raccoon getting ready to steal a pie from a kitchen, to make sure nobody was listening, and then he told me a little.

I guess you heard about them what they called Tong Wars in New York when a couple of hundred Chinamen killed each other with hatchets. Well, it was the same here in Menang, only a thousand times worse. And they had the craziest names for a gang you ever heard of, The Society of Harmonious Daggers, and The Society of Graceful Accomplishments, and The Celestial Tigers, and The Heaven on Earth Society, and I don't know what all. And the worse the society was, the prettier name it had.

I talked about it some more to Bertie when I stopped at the Four Elephants for a drink. He looked more like a jockey than ever when he's there in his place; he's so small his head don't come much over the bar. He fixes himself a chew of betel nut—that's the stuff all the natives out there use, turns your teeth black and makes you spit red—and chucks it into his mouth.

"The societies take over the bloomin' politics, too," he says. "The island's run by a Malay they call a bloomin' Tunku, and they cook up a plot and throw out the old Tunku and put in a new one, looks like, every couple of months. The one they got now is a doddering old bloke, kind of half-witted, and the real boss is his playboy brother. If you get around the amusement park they call the Happy World you're sure to see him. He's got eight or ten wives already. But he goes there all the time looking for new ones. He's a real bloomin' snake in the grass."

Alf, the bartender, who'd been busy tossing a drunk out the door like he was a sack of potatoes, nods his bull head. "People hate the Tunku's bloody brother like a Swede sailor hates to drink water. They'd get rid of him and the bloody Tunku in a minute if it wasn't for the Harmonious Daggers, they're the biggest secret society right now. The brother gives 'em the chance to make all the crooked money they want, so 'course they're all for him. They're the ones did the kidnaping. They ride around on bloody green bicycles, and have daggers hid inside the bloody bicycle pumps. They'll kill a man for you for five dollars and give you trading stamps."

He hurries off as the drunk comes in the doorway again.

"Everything he told you is bloomin' right," says Bertie. "You say Harmonious Daggers to a rich Chinese and in a second he's all covered with goose pimples like he's a bloomin' gooseberry bush. All the rich Chinese got triple electric fences around their houses, and Great Danes big as lions that can eat a man quicker than they can swallow a bloomin' hamburger. Don't be too scared if some Harmonious Dagger fellows come around on the bicycles, and just stand there awhile. They're just looking you over, the way they do everybody. Like I said they ain't bothered us Eng-

lishmen yet. But if they stop standing and come to talk to
you, get ready to leave this bloomin' island fast. . . . Alf,
before you throw that bloomin' drunk out again, take out
his false teeth, will you? I just remembered he owes us six
dollars from yesterday."

Funny thing, it was almost as if those Chinamen heard us
talking. Because a few days later they came up to the boat,
three little Chinese riding their green bicycles. They stood
out on the wharf for half a hour, I guess, just looking. And
pretty soon the same big black car that I seen the day the
rubber merchant was kidnaped drove up, and a tall Chinese
fellow with black sword moustaches and wearing a black
suit like a undertaker stepped out. He had the meanest face
I ever saw, looked just like Dr. Fu Manchu in the comic
book they had about him. It was a fine one, that Fu Manchu
comic.

This fellow walked up to the men on the bicycles and
spoke to them a minute, and then drove off in the car again.

Mock Duck watched him go and his face got all goose
flesh between the wrinkles, like the rich men Alf was talking about.

"The gods of the temple told you not to start this school,
Tuan," he kind of moaned. "But you would not listen. This
is the chief of the Harmonious Daggers. He is the wickedest
man in all Menang. I do not know what evil he will do."

The fellows with the bicycles stayed there maybe a hour,
and then they rode away.

They came every day after that. But nothing happened.
Like Bertie said, it seemed like they was just looking us
over.

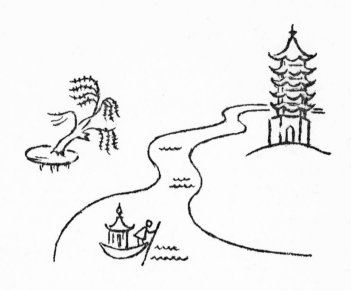

Chapter III

We had the school just about ready at
last and set the date for the opening. We put up more signs
in the big room, *Every Day In Mind And Body I'm Getting
Stronger And Stronger*, *There's Always A Way To Win*,
and things like that that G.B. got out of the book. And
then we put up pictures on the wall of all the people in the
world that had done big things, Julius Caesar, and Napoleon, and George Washington, and Abe Lincoln, and people like that. Right in the middle we had the crossed flags of
the United States and Menang and over these a new *Every
Man A King* sign, bigger than any of the others. Near this
was a picture G.B. had cut from a magazine of the statues
of the Presidents carved on that mountain out in the Black
Hills of South Dakota. And then for the ladies a picture of
a pretty girl wearing a white dress and a golden crown that

was Miss America, with a sign underneath saying, *This Could Be You.*

We fixed it so G.B.'d teach what they call the success classes, and I'd take care of the place, doing the painting and carpenter work and things like that you always need on a boat. And we figured besides the success things they'd like to know about America. I'd always been crazy about history in the little bit of school I had, and I had a American history Pa gave me the year before he gave me the dictionary, told all about the Pilgrims, and Captain John Smith and Pocahontas, and the Mexican War and things like that. It was a regular book, not a comic book. I'd brought it with me, because I never let that book go.

Pa's father'd give it to him like the dictionary, and it had a beautiful flag on the cover. The flag had only forty-six stars for forty-six states, and I'd look at it plenty of times and think how now there were fifty, and how wonderful it is the way America's growing.

Besides that regular book I had a few of the Great History comics I'd bought when I was in the Army, and G.B. thought it'd be nice if I taught the students some American history. And course I liked that fine.

Well, a few days before the school was to start, G.B. fixed up a loudspeaker on a old truck we hired and I drove it around town. And then when we come to a good place we'd stop, and Mu Lan that was riding up front with us and Mock Duck and Amok that were riding behind would get down and pass out some nice looking bills we'd had printed. We got plenty of people around us fast, because G.B. had the speaker tuned up so loud everybody ran out of their houses, thinking it was a air raid. Deaf people that hadn't heard a sound for twenty years heard it, they said. If it'd been any louder it would have knocked down some buildings. I tell you that G.B. never missed a trick.

Bertie came over to see the place the night before the

opening. "It looks wonderful," he said. "It's so bloomin' good wouldn't take much to make me sign up myself. If I'd have taken a course like that maybe I'd be farther than I am today. That's why you bloomin' Americans get where you do, you're always having ideas."

Well in the morning we were up at five o'clock, putting on what they call the finishing touches. Mu Lan came in her red and gold silk coat and trousers, and Mock Duck and Amok had shirts they'd washed so shiny white when you looked at them you had to blink your eyes. First thing we did was hang up strings of firecrackers. Mock Duck said the noise would scare away any demons that wanted to come around, trying to bring us bad luck. And then a boy came carrying a wreath saying "Success To Success. From A Friend." I wondered who it came from, and then I found out G.B. sent it himself. Like I said, he was always thinking up something smart like that. And then he put a gold ribbon across the door so he could cut it, like when the Congressman opens a new road or something back home. And then we tested out the loudspeaker to make sure it was working, and waited.

We sure didn't have long to wait. By ten o'clock there was a big crowd on the bank, and by twelve, when we were going to open I'll bet there were a couple of thousand people, Malays, and Chinese, and Hindus packed so thick they were like sardines after you poured the oil out of the can.

I was really scared when I looked at them. "I didn't expect nothing like this," I said to G.B. "This boat won't hold more than 500 people. Don't let 'em all in at once or they'll sink us sure."

"That's sure right," says G.B. "We'll let 'em on 200 at a time. You stay here and count 'em and I'll show 'em around the boat."

Well, Mock Duck lit the firecrackers and they went off like it was the *Maine* blowing up. And then G.B. made a speech on the loudspeaker, saying how glad he was to be able to open the school in a fine place like Menang. And then Mu Lan gave him a scissors all covered over with gold paint, and he cut the ribbon, and invited the first 200 people to come aboard. I expected a big mob of them to come rushing forward, and got ready for a terrible time to hold them back.

But not a single soul of them moved.

"That's funny," says G.B. "I guess the speaker ain't working right. I'll tune it up louder."

He tunes it up so it must have blowed the rocks off the mountains ten miles away. But everybody stands stiff as dead people, waiting for a undertaker to put them in their coffins.

G.B. is getting desperate and grabs hold of Mock Duck. "Maybe they don't understand English. You tell 'em in Chinese."

Mock Duck does what he says. But still they don't wink an eyelash. Not one of them comes aboard.

Pretty soon when they see nothing is going to happen they begin moving away. And before long of the 2000 people, not a single one is left.

Bertie, who'd come for a few minutes from the bar, took a chew of betel nut, and spit over the side in disgust. "That's the trouble with this bloomin' country. It's the bloomin' mysteries. Things happen all the time and you never find out why."

And Mock Duck looked black as a tornado and said he knowed it'd be that way when the gods told us not to open the school.

We sat around all day like we were at a funeral.

In the middle of the afternoon, we're in the big room when Mu Lan came running to say two Americans were coming aboard. Well, two Americans ain't exactly the crowd we've been expecting, but they're better than nothing, so we go out to meet them.

They were two American sailors in fancy white uniforms off the warship come into the harbor that morning. Tough looking fellows these were, not like most sailors, nice and easy.

G.B. hurries up to them. "I'm sure glad to see you, buddies," he says.

They don't waste no time with him.

"Where's the girls?" says the oldest one, with a voice that'd sandpaper iron.

"Girls? What girls, buddies?" says G.B.

"Girls. Skirts. Broads," says the one with the sandpaper voice.

"Femmes. Dolls. Dames," grunts the other, hunching up his shoulders as if he's getting ready to fight.

G.B. shakes his head kind of puzzled. "There ain't no girls here, buddies."

They both give him a funny look.

"Ain't this a loveboat?" says the sandpaper one.

"This is a school, buddies," says G.B., kind of dignified.

"A . . . what?" says the one with the hunched shoulders.

"A school. . . . To develop your personality, buddies."

"Christ on a life raft," says the sailors together, and they go down the gangplank and onto the shore.

And we sat like we were at the funeral again.

Amok was as superstitious as Mock Duck, and ever since the priest had given us the warning he'd been looking upset, and I was getting worried about him. And this morning, after the crowd didn't come on, he looked terrible. I'd heard from Alf it was when things went wrong that the amuck people got bad; so I guess I was watching him close. It was pretty near sunset, I guess, and I'm sitting in the big room by myself, when he goes past and I see his eyes are getting glassy. And all of a sudden I see him dash to the kitchen, and grab a big knife hanging over the sink.

"He's going to run amuck!" shouts Mu Lan, who was at the stove cooking, and she races to get out of the way.

I jump up and make what they call a flying tackle for him, and get him pinned down to the floor. I hold him there maybe five minutes while he's wriggling and struggling in his kind of lady's skirt to get away; and pretty soon he quiets down, and I can see he's all right again. And he began to cry and say how sorry he was; and the scar under his eye fills with tears again and he tells me how he'd die if I fired him. And then G.B. that'd been on the bank came in, and I had to tell him what happened. Like I figured, he wanted to fire Amok right off. But I argued with him about it not being Amok's fault he was born a Bugi, and his being such a wonderful fellow other times, so G.B. said we'd let him stay.

It was sure a fine way to open a school.

We'd sent off Mock Duck to see if he could find out any reason why the people didn't come aboard. He was away all day, and we began to wonder what had happened. It got dark, and Mu Lan fixed us a supper, though nobody felt like eating a bite. We'd just sat down at the table when we hear footsteps running along the bank; in a minute Mock Duck comes busting in, all excited like a raccoon that's just robbed a beehive, and panting for breath.

"I have found out, O Tuans!" he calls to both of us. "It is the Feng Shui!"

"The what?" says G.B.

"The Feng Shui. The spirits. There are very bad Feng Shui here. The boat moored at the dock before this one burned in the night and killed many people. And on the boat before that the captain was hung by the police; and his wife killed her seven children and then cut her throat. The man who rented this boat to you is very evil, O Tuans. No one in Menang would rent a boat in a place with such a fearful Feng Shui. Only foreigners like you. That is why the people will not come aboard. They are afraid something terrible will happen."

I thought he was crazy, but when we stopped in at the Four Elephants that night, Alf said Mock Duck sure was right.

"This Feng Shui's the biggest thing in all the bloody Chinese religion," he roars, slapping out half a dozen beers to a bunch of Russian sailors, like a cook in a wagon diner dishing out pancakes. "Bertie had to move this pub twice before he got somewhere the bloody Chinese'd come to. There was a piece in the Singapore paper a couple of weeks ago how they'd had to take off the whole top story of a bloody new skyscraper in Hong Kong because the bloody Feng Shui up there was wrong."

Bertie slices off a new supply of betel, and jams it into his mouth that's all red with the juice. "You can't lift a finger here without the bloomin' Feng Shui. I should have told you. You ask Mock Duck to get you a Feng Shui professor and he'll show you the right place. . . . Alf, stop that Russki and that German from fighting, will you? One ear bit off in a week's plenty. And a ear's hard to find on a floor."

Well, we sent out Mock Duck first thing next morning, and he came back in a little while with a funny humpbacked little Chinaman so old he looked like the fellow back home they called Whistling Jimmie that said he'd been living 135 years and could remember seeing George Washington. The Chinaman carried what he called a compass, though it sure wasn't like any compass I ever saw on a ship, and a bag of cow bones. And he did a lot of rigamarole with the compass, and heated the bones over the stove. And he studied the cracks in them for a while, and then he turned to us.

37

"This place has the worst Feng Shui I have seen and I have lived many years, Tuans," he says, in a high squeaky voice cracked worse than the bones. "One of the hills behind the city even you who are not Chinese can see is shaped like a dragon. And your boat blocks the dragon's view out to sea, and makes the dragon very angry. This, Tuans, would be evil enough, for an angry dragon is No. 2 in the calendar of evil Feng Shui, which some professors number up to 1004, but to those more learned like myself, are numbered up to 2097."

He put the bones in a leather pouch. "But the dragon is not the worst, Tuans. The great evil is that your boat rests over a turtle who died here fifty years ago and now lies at the bottom of the sea. Each time today when the spirit of the turtle wishes to rise it bumps against the bottom of your boat. And this naturally makes it very angry, even angrier than the dragon. And in the calendar of evil Feng Shui an angry turtle is numbered one."

Well, he fooled around with the compass again, and showed us where to move the boat, maybe a couple of hundred yards down the shore. And then he said to wait seven days and then on the afternoon of the seventh day to open up the school again at four minutes after two.

Well, I know it sounds crazy, but we moved it like he said, and waited for the week to pass.

And the fellows on the green bicycles rode up every morning and stayed watching on the bank like they'd done before, and then they went away.

A couple of days after we moved a Chinese holiday came along they call The Feast of the Lanterns. Mu Lan had been working awful hard, and I thought it'd be nice to take her to the Happy World that Bertie had talked about, the little park at the edge of town. Course I couldn't take her by herself; those Chinese girls are terrible strict. So her married sister said she'd come along, a nice, stout little lady wearing green pajamas and kind of giggling all the time. I took a trishaw to where they lived with Mock Duck, in one of the bunches of little houses on stilts built over the water. In the streets everybody was carrying paper lanterns, big lanterns shaped like tigers and dragons, and little lanterns shaped like stars and moons. We got to the stilt houses after a while; I guess there were a couple of hundred. They were built all together with narrow plank walks in between, full of holes so big you pretty near fell through. You had to be a trapeze performer to walk ten feet. But every house had a lantern in the window, and it was real pretty.

It was hard to find Mu Lan's place, but I kept going on the plank walks and pretty soon I was there. Mu Lan and her sister were waiting for me, the sister in chunky purple pajamas this time, and Mu Lan all dressed up in her red and gold coat and trousers, with gold earrings big as a dollar pretty near, and an orchid in her hair, like her name. She sure looked beautiful.

We took the trishaw again and started off to the Happy World. Mu Lan at first was kind of quiet and bashful, because she'd never been out like this before; but her sister was giggling all the time.

We got to the Happy World pretty quick and I seen right away it wasn't like the one in Singapore; that one is like Coney Island pretty near, with rides and picture shows. This one was a quiet little place, looked like another scene on the china plates my uncle brought Ma back from the war. There were thirteen of the plates, twelve in the dozen, and then they gave you the one extra, that made the dozen thirteen. The plate I'm talking about had a little blue river painted on it, with blue weeping willow trees and a couple of blue bridges, and the Happy World was the same way. You could sit in a little dragon boat and row yourself under the bridges, past little blue pagodas and things. And there were gold pheasants and peacocks everywhere, showing off their tails. I guess the fellow that painted the plate must have come to the park sometime.

The park was full of lanterns, too, and in a few minutes after we went through the gate, Mu Lan forgot her bashfulness and was all excited. And when I rented one of the dragon boats and started rowing her and her sister along the little river, her face got like the pictures I seen on Sunday School cards, when a lady that becomes a saint dies and finds out she's going to Heaven. Sometimes she'd clap her little hands, and you'd swear it was a doll running by clockwork again; and then she'd start talking so fast you couldn't understand half of what she was saying. And then, all of a sudden she'd get all quiet and just stand there shivering. And I'd be worried for a minute and then I'd see she was shivering because she was so happy.

Her sister sat by us fanning herself, because it was a real hot night; and then every once in a while she'd start to giggle and she'd hide her face behind the fan.

Well, they had a elephant there you could ride, and we tried to get the sister up on him. But she was too fat and too scared, so Mu Lan and me did it together. Mu Lan was a little scared, too, but it was sure nice sitting there close by her, with the elephant's big ears waggling and his trunk swishing up and down. Once the elephant gave a sudden lurch and Mu Lan almost fell off. I caught her quick around the waist, and pulled her back and made sure she was safe again. And she felt so soft and delicate it was like you were touching a feather. And then her eyes got a look, kind of happy, kind of sad, like a old dog gives you after you been away a long time and you've just come back.

After that we sat drinking tea under the weeping willows with the big peacocks strutting around; and we watched some beautiful Malay girls dancing in a open air theater, like they were statues all covered with gold. And the music for them was made by Malay fellows playing the gongs; it sounded kind of like a calliope on a excursion steamboat on the Mississippi at Memphis.

We left pretty soon after that, because the park was closing, and I took them back in a trishaw. And I walked with them to the door of the house, and the sister giggled and made what they call a curtsy. And Mu Lan made a curtsy, too, and then her eyes got all soft again, like the old dog when you've come back.

And then all of a sudden she ran inside and came out with something and put it in my hand. "To remember when I was falling," she said. And I looked, and it was a little ivory elephant.

We sure had a wonderful time.

Well, we printed some new bills for Mu Lan and the others to pass out, and went with the loudspeaker in the truck again, inviting everybody to the new opening. And pretty soon it was four minutes after two on the seventh day, and a crowd was waiting on the bank, even bigger than before. Mock Duck shot off the firecrackers, and G.B. made a speech again and cut the ribbon with the gold scissors. And I know it sounds crazy, but now the people come on by the hundreds to look around the boat and the school.

I never seen so many people in one place before and so much excitement since the time I was a kid when they put up the war monument in Muleshoe, and a big general came and pulled back the curtain covering it, and there was a warship and a cannon and a airplane, and three soldiers standing by, saluting a big American flag.

There were so many people on the boat once it kind of started to tip over, and I was really afraid it was going to sink. So we had to make some of the people get off for a while.

Well, they kept coming and coming long after dark, and they didn't stop till midnight.

And when the last one was gone we counted the cards

we'd filled out for the people that was going to join the classes. There were thirty-six and we hadn't counted on more than twenty.

G.B. took hold of everybody there, me and Mu Lan and Mock Duck and Amok, who was feeling all right now; and he waltzed us around until we were dizzy.

He stops the dancing all of a sudden, out of breath. "You heard of people walking on their heads for joy," he said. "You're going to see it right now."

And in a second he's standing upside down, and bumping on his head across the floor. And being a little bit heavy-set the way he was it shakes the whole room.

That was the thing about G.B. You never knew what he was going to do next.

He stands up again and gets serious for a minute. "I knew it was going to be big," he says. "But I never figured on anything like this. It's the biggest thing since the automobile."

He looks out the window where you can see the rubber warehouse and the other buildings on the bank shining in the moonlight. "You mark my words. This school's going to change this town so in a couple of years nobody'll know it's the same place. Because like it says there on the sign I'm going to make every man here a king."

Chapter IV

We told everybody the classes'd start next day, a little before sunset. We figured it'd be better that way so people could come after they got through working.

The fellows on the green bicycles hadn't been around for a while, but when we woke up that morning, there they were on the bank again, four of them this time.

"I wish those fellows wouldn't stay around here," I said to G.B., who was shaving extra fancy. "They sure make me nervous."

"I ain't worried a bit," says G.B. "You know what Bertie said. They're just looking us over and looking's cheap as fleas at a dog show. If they don't bother a Englishman they sure won't bother us."

The four Chinamen rode away after a little while and I stopped thinking about them.

The students started arriving at 5:30, and each person G.B. slapped on the back and gave them a button we'd fixed up, like the buttons they wore in the Rotary Club I seen that time when I went down for the Amateur Hour. The first fellow that came was a Hindu, a big, jolly fellow like G.B., different than most other Hindus that look like they're on the way to the cemetery for their own funeral and they ain't able to pay for the grave. He owned a little barber shop near the boat, and his name was Gunga Das.

G.B. pins a button on him. "You'll be Gunga Din in the school," he says. And he busts out with a big laugh. "You're a better man than I am, Gunga Din," and slaps him on the back again. It was sure smart of G.B. to think about that poem. It suited this fellow just right.

The next man was a little Thai fellow that was a Buddhist monk, wearing a yellow silk robe, hardly said a word; when he did talk it was like he was afraid the police was listening. His name was Tak Thong—that's a Thai name— and G.B. pinned a button on him the way he did the Hindu, and busts out laughing again. "We'll just call you plain Tack," he says. "That's a name kind of sticks into you."

Well, he did this with all thirty-six of them, with a different funny name for each one. There'd have been thirty-seven except one of them, a little gray-haired Chinese lady in a black dress when we asked her what she did said she ran a loveboat, and we didn't think with a high-class kind of school like this it'd be so good.

Course there weren't any really big people, like bankers, and doctors, and rich men owned factories, and things like that I'd kind of hoped would come. These were all kind of sad-looking people made you feel kind of sad, too, seeing them. I guess most of them were what you call kind of failures, or they wouldn't have come. But they were all right.

44

They were nice. And they sure needed us to help them. Besides Gunga Das and Tak they were mostly kind of dried up Chinese and Malay clerks worked in the rubber warehouses; and a rubber tapper, and a couple of plain Chinese girls wearing thick glasses made them look like owls, that worked as secretaries, all wanting better jobs, I guess. And there was a big fellow with a face looked like he was crying all the time, said he worked as a mourner that walked along with other mourners in Chinese funerals.

There was a big Indian, the kind they call a Sikh with big shiny moustaches, said he wanted to be a bank guard, the way most of the Sikhs are in Singapore, but he never could get any confidence in himself. And there was one old Chinaman, I guess had a little money maybe, said he wanted to get enough confidence to get married. He was seventy his last birthday, he said, but if you ain't married the Chinese treat you like a child and send you packages of candy wrapped in red paper, and things like that at New Year's, just the way they do little kids; and he was getting tired of it.

There was a little Malay worked in the place where they had Chinese boxing, sweeping up, had always wanted to be a boxer, but he didn't have any confidence, either. And he'd found a pocketbook one night after the fights, and thought he'd spend the money going to the school. I talked it over with G.B. and we gave him a special low rate.

Well, they all sat down on the chairs before the desk where G.B was standing. Their faces were all lighted up now, waiting for him to begin, kind of like flowers when the sun's just coming out after a hard rain.

He hits a big gong he's got there, and waits a minute till they're all quiet. And then all of a sudden he jumps up on top of the desk, scattering the papers on it all over.

"I want everybody that comes to this school to jump to his work like a tiger!" he shouts.

Like I said, you never could tell what G.B. was going to do.

All the people there get terrible worried, because they can't figure out what's going on. And then G.B. laughs, and jumps down again.

"Don't be scared," he says. "I ain't going crazy. Most people in Menang are too easy going. That's why they ain't got any farther. I want to shock you into action, till you're quick as a tiger."

He starts talking then and goes on and on like a Hardshell Baptist preacher. Only G.B. was really saying something all the time. He talked to them about what they call inspiration, and asks them if they can afford to lose a million dollars, because that's what maybe they'll lose if they don't develop their personality. And he takes a wooden pointer and shows them the sign on the wall, *You Are The Master Of Your Fate; Fate Is Not The Master Of You,* and tells them how if they want something bad enough and think about it hard enough, they can do it, no matter what.

And he points to the statues of the Presidents cut out of the Black Hills, and he says everybody sitting there in front of him can be carved out of a mountain the same way. Sometimes he talks all excited and sometimes kind of in a whisper, like you talk in a house where somebody died. He was sure a wonderful speaker. Like I said, he could have been one of the Presidents carved there if he'd have put his mind to it.

The room got so quiet you could almost have heard a couple of big ants that was near the desk, walking across the floor. And he picks up the wooden pointer again, and touches it to the sign over the flags, *Every Man A King.*

"Remember these words," he says. "I want you to always see 'em before you in letters red as fire. It's the motto of this school. Now please say them after me, slowly. Every man and woman can be a king and queen."

Well, of course by now he had them eating out of his hands; and they began chanting the words over and over.

With their soft voices it was like when you pass a Catholic church and you hear the preachers there singing in what they call Latin.

Well, he went on like this for a hour, telling them how the best way to get confidence is to make speeches, and how Demosthenes was the greatest speaker of them all, and made his first speeches with his mouth full of stones. And then he picks up a glass jar full of pebbles, and makes some of the people put the pebbles in their mouths and make speeches like Demosthenes, and pretty soon everybody's mumbling away and having a fine time.

And then he tells them he wants them to take setting-up exercises, and I teach them the exercises I learned in the Army. And when they get through he makes them say over and over, "Every day in mind and body I'm getting stronger and stronger." And they go around humming the words the way they did before.

And then he walks to the door like a preacher down South when he's finished his sermon, and shakes hands with everybody as they start going out the door, and I tell you in the couple of hours they were there you could see they were almost changed people. There was a different look in their eyes, and they even seemed to be standing straighter.

Next night a couple of the fellows that had been so meek-looking came to the class carrying big krisses, and we had a hard time making them put the knives away, because we didn't want any fights.

"They're learning too bloody fast," roars Alf in the bar one afternoon, when we'd been going a couple of weeks. "These little fellows got brains quick as a bloody mouse-trap. There's a little Chinaman comes in here all the time that's taking your bloody course now, used to run if a mynah feather come blowin' toward him. Last night a big Pole called him what sounded like a dirty name in Polak, and the bloody little Chinaman knocked him so cold you could have used him to ice fish. When the Polak come to, after a couple of hours he said we ain't running a nice place, where you let somebody hit a man with a axe."

Well, every time the people come, G.B. had something different for them. He'd get one of the students to talk on the loudspeaker and then he'd tell some other student to speak so their voices would drown the loudspeaker out. And he kept tuning it louder and louder till you could have heard the people making their speeches off in Fiji, pretty near. And then one night he put a old brass lamp on the table, and told them to imagine it was Aladdin's lamp and to come up and touch it and make a wish, and if they wished hard enough, that was the way it'd be. Course they were terrible superstitious, even the smartest ones, and that made a big hit too. You could generally always see somebody going around, humming to himself that about every day I'm getting stronger and stronger, and then he'd go up and put a finger on the lamp.

One night a week G.B. gave them talks on How to Become a Millionaire and how to get ahead in business. And they were the biggest hit of all. And he took the personality book that come from the States and he fixed up another little book from it, taking the main points and leaving out the trash, and printed his name on it so nobody'd get the book he wrote mixed up with the other fellow's. And he gave one of his books to everybody in the class. And all the people that was studying at the school began talking to all their friends, and the friends came, too. And pretty soon we had more people than we knew what to do with. I tell you things were sure booming.

There wasn't as many took the history course as I'd figured. There was only three or four come to each class, and that was counting Mu Lan. She come every time. But I sure enjoyed it.

Mock Duck and Mu Lan had to go away for a couple of days to another part of the island where a cousin or somebody died, and Mock Duck asked me to be sure to give the Kitchen God the betel nut he got every day while Mock Duck was gone. I said I'd do it but I forgot.

The second night Mock Duck was away a traveling theater gave a show on the shore, what they call a Chinese opera, where people dressed like kings and queens and generals go around hitting each other with swords and spears; they scream like a bunch of cats electing a president. I stayed watching a while, and the people living in the neighborhood brought their god from the temple, a nice, fat little idol to see the show, just like he was a human. They gave him the best place, and come around him every few minutes, I guess to see how he was enjoying the acts. And it made me remember how I'd forgot about Mock Duck and the Kitchen God, and I said to myself I'd give him the betel nut soon as I went back to the boat. But when I walked over Mock Duck already was back from the country, and had made a special trip to see the god, and was waiting for me. He was looking black as a raccoon when he finds another raccoon's stole some apples that he's been hiding.

"O Tuan, this is a sorry thing you have done," he tells me, almost crying. "The Kitchen God will be burning with anger at you, Tuan, and at me also. And when the Kitchen God is angry something terrible will happen. I will go to the temple and pray."

That was what once in a while kind of drove you crazy. Some little thing would come up you'd think was a joke pretty near, and it'd turn out it was more important than living or dying.

The fellows on the green bicycles had stopped coming again after the opening day, and I'd pretty near forgot about them, when a few days later I see them come racing to the wharf. A few minutes after, the big black car drives up, and stops right in front of the boat. The door opens and out steps the fellow in the undertaker suit looks just like Fu Manchu.

He walks up the gangplank stiff as if he's got one of them long Chinese spears in his back. G.B.'s up town doing a errand so I hurry to meet him.

He lights a cigarette like he owns the place.

"Who's in charge here?" he says, talking almost like he'd been in the States, but the way he said the words were more like the English society dudes you see in the moving pictures. He was sure nasty.

"I'm one of the bosses," I say, still kind of polite. "What you want?"

"I came to do you a favor," says Fu Manchu, smoking his cigarette like the smart-aleck dudes in the pictures. "Menang has many unscrupulous men who always watch when things are going well with an enterprise as it is with your school, and sometimes wish to share in the profits. If provoked they might rob you or burn your boat or perhaps even kill you."

He points off to the fellows on the bicycles. "My friends there would like to look after you, so you will have no difficulties."

"Here's your hat, what's your hurry," I say, talking like I knew G.B. would talk if he'd been there, though of course I didn't have his hat to give him.

Mock Duck and Amok come hurrying out from the kitchen, looking awful nervous. Mock Duck pulls me off to one side.

"O Tuan, Tuan, I knew this evil would come to you," he whispers. "It is because of what you have done to the Kitchen God. This chief of the Harmonious Daggers is the friend of the Tunku's brother. If he wishes he can have us all killed before morning. Please do what he says, Tuan."

He sees I ain't paying any attention and goes back with Amok into the kitchen, his face the color of one of the big lilies people put on a coffin.

The fellow in the undertaker suit smiles, the kind of smile Fu Manchu has in the comic book when he's going to put the detective following him to the rat torture or something. "It will not be expensive," he says. "We try to make the charges to our clients reasonable."

My Kentucky temper is red hot now. "Get out," I tell him.

And he goes down the gangplank in a hurry.

Mock Duck and Amok come out of the kitchen, and watch the car drive down the shore. A few minutes later I see Mock Duck kneeling in front of the Kitchen God, and then he gets up and gives the god all the little pieces of candied ginger he was saving—he was as crazy about ginger as a cat is about catnip—and I knew he'd never have done that unless he was worried to death.

G.B. come back a little later and I told him about everything. And he said I'd done just right.

Nothing happened next day or the day after that or the next week either. So G.B. and me figured Fu Manchu'd been scared off, and we forgot about him.

The school kept on doing fine. Everybody worked hard, and a lot of the people stayed after hours, studying the little book G.B. wrote and talking things over with him and me. And I sure was happy.

The students was getting on wonderful. You could see the changes in them every day, the way they were getting more confidence. The Chinese girls had begun taking off their glasses part of the time, and they were real pretty. And the old Chinese that was seventy said his relatives had sent him some kid's presents the way they always did, and he'd sent them right back; and he was beginning to look at the girls plenty. And even the little Malay that swept up in the boxing place said they were going to let him have a chance to box once in a while with the beginning fellows nobody knew, before the big matches started.

The little gray-haired lady that ran the loveboat kept coming back, asking to join the school. She said her business had been falling off, and maybe she could get some good ideas. And she was so kind of old and quiet and begged so hard, we give in at last. And she'd sit off by herself, listening to G.B. talk, and studying the book, not talking to anybody, and then she'd go on home. I talked to her and she come to the history class a couple of times, but she didn't keep it up some way.

The best of all the students were Tak Thong, the Buddhist monk, and Gunga Das, had the barber shop. Every night you'd see them going around with the stones in their mouths, giving Lincoln's Gettysburg Address or Marc Antony's speech at Caesar's funeral.

Tak had been wanting us to come out to see his temple, but we didn't have the time. And then one day I saw a big calico tomcat meowing on the bank, looking terrible hungry, so I took him in and gave him some milk, and he acted so pitiful I decided to keep him on the boat. And Tak told me they were having a special service for cats—they have church for animals in their temples same as humans—and he said why didn't I come and bring the cat, too, and I could christen him the way they do people. So I put the cat in a basket and went with Mu Lan and her sister.

It was a beautiful temple, with a Sleeping Buddha as big as the Empire State Building in New York. Temple bells were tinkling everywhere, and the Thai monks like Tak were going around in yellow robes, chanting their prayers and counting their beads, and the Chinese monks were doing the same, dressed all in red. And all of them were wearing the biggest hats I ever saw, with brims maybe a foot and a half wide.

We put the cat by the big Buddha with a lot of other cats—he was getting fattened up now and tough, like he'd been listening to the talks at the school—and we had to hold him tight to keep him from clawing a couple of toms standing by him. I christened him Chang because that was the name of the Chinaman that spit on the shirts in Muleshoe. And then when him and the other cats were blessed, Tak took us around to see the rest of the temple and the temple gardens. Tak's face wasn't sad like when he first came to the school; and now he was beginning to talk plenty.

It was a beautiful place, with pools covered all over by what they call lotus and full of goldfish big as your arm, and wonderful flowers smelled so sweet it almost knocked you down. It was the quietest place in the world, I guess. When a frog jumped in one of the pools, it sounded so loud you thought someone fired a cannon.

Right in the middle was a big pigeon house, with maybe five hundred pigeons flying and strutting around, and the cat went crazy trying to get them. The pigeons were real scared; the Menang people said if they ever flew away something awful would happen to the town, like the big volcano that was in the middle of the island blowing up, or a terrible tidal wave.

But I understood now why Tak looked so thin. The temple was terrible poor. The pigeons was the only ones eating. The other monks were even skinnier than Tak; they were only allowed to eat one meal a day. They got a little money carving beautiful Buddhas out of ivory, but one of the statues took six months to make, so they couldn't make very many. They were having a little fair in the temple grounds to raise some money the way they do there, with little booths where you could buy the Buddhas and prayer books, and little chunks of peanut candy; but there weren't more than six or seven people that had come to the whole fair.

We met what they called the abbot, a Chinese with a face looked like one of them old-time saints; he wouldn't walk at night when it was cool, because he was afraid he'd step on a ant or something and kill it in the dark. And he looked hungrier than anybody.

He had maybe a dozen pretty birds he'd bought in the market, and he was opening the doors of the cages the people had kept them in so they could go free.

"It is beautiful, the life of a monk," he says to me in a voice so soft it's like touching velvet. "We have little. But we study and pray. And the gods are kind. In this temple we are very close to Heaven."

We left him, and Tak's face got mournful again, like it was the day of the opening.

"O Tuan, it is very sad here," he says. "We live on the rice and the money we get by begging. Often the rice is full of insects and sometimes a lizard, and the money is not even a penny. It is this way because we must wear these large hats so that when a person puts his gift into our bowl we must look down at Mother Earth and the brim hangs so far down it covers our eyes and we cannot see what he is giving."

He looked off where the abbot was opening another cage, and got a queer look in his eye. "The abbot is a good man. But he spends all the money feeding the pigeons and buying the birds in the market; so the monks go hungry. Some day perhaps I will become the abbot, and there will be many changes. That is what I am learning at the school, Tuan."

I took Mu Lan and her sister and Chang back in a trishaw. Mu Lan and me was getting really friendly now. The more I saw of her, the better I liked her with her cute little ways and everything. I stopped at their house on stilts for tea before I went back to the boat. I hadn't really seen it the time we went to the Happy World. But now I got a good look, and it was really nice, all fixed up with piles of pretty pillow cushions and red and gold curtains. I sat on the floor, by a little table, and when she poured the tea with her little hands, it was like you were inside a doll's house and were being served by a doll.

We went out a lot together to the beach, and for little boat rides on the river. And once we went to the volcano; that's the big sight on the island where all the tourists off the cruise boats go. It took a hour to get there over a bad road but it was worth the trouble; when you looked into the crater, all bubbling and sizzling with flames and hot rocks shooting up, it was like you were looking into hell. Like Japan girls threw themselves in when they were disappointed in love.

Mu Lan's dead mother had a uncle that was pretty rich —he made the paper models they burned at funerals—and he liked Mu Lan and her sister. And he was having a big party for his being seventy-eight years old, and invited them to come. And Mu Lan, knowing how I liked to learn about things that way, got it fixed so I could come along.

The party was at night, and when we get there I see a big wall, with a lot of people going through a big gate, and hear a lot of firecrackers going off on the other side. We follow the people into a courtyard and then into a courtyard ain't so big, and then a courtyard still smaller. It was like those Chinese boxes you take out one after another and they keep getting littler and littler; till you finally get to the last one, ain't much bigger than a dice. And all the courtyards were crowded with hundreds of kids running around, all dressed up for the birthday. And they were shooting off the firecrackers we'd heard, and spit-devils and rockets and a funny kind of Roman candles.

Mu Lan took me to meet the uncle, a old fellow had a skin kind of like the diploma I seen in the doctor's office the time I hurt my arm at the filling station in Memphis; the diploma was all crinkled up and was made of what they call parchment. He couldn't talk a word of English because he was a old-fashioned Chinese; and he bowed and I bowed like Mu Lan told me, and he smiled and shook my hand. And Mu Lan told him I had the school on the boat, and he bowed again, very low; because that's a big thing with the Chinese, anything to do with education. And then he showed me a picture of all his children and grandchildren and there were a hundred and twenty people in it. And then he pointed and said something to Mu Lan and she told me about fifty were missing.

And then we all sat down at a big table in one of the courtyards, and it had places, I guess, for a couple of hundred people. There were maybe a hundred different kinds of Chinese food, you never seen anything like it. There were sharks' fins, and birds' nest soup, and steamed fish, and sweet and sour pork, and butterfly shrimp, and maybe ten kinds of chicken. But it all stayed there on the table; nobody started eating.

"They're waiting till somebody says, 'Grandfather, eat rice,'" Mu Lan tells me.

And just then a little kid wasn't more than three stands up, and says "Grandfather, please eat rice. Granduncle, please eat rice. Grandaunt, please eat rice."

And he kept it up, saying father, mother, elder brother, second brother, please eat rice, till he'd mentioned all the family. Then the next kid, this one about six years old, does just the same, and the next and the next, till everybody at the table pretty near has said please eat rice to all the people older than them. I guess it took about half an hour before they all got through. And I was sure getting hungry and beginning to think we'd starve to death. And then we started eating, and it was sure worth waiting for.

Mu Lan gave me a pair of chopsticks, and I did pretty good. Once I reached for a piece of shark's fin with them, but she touched my hand.

"It is too big, Tuan," she said. "If you tried to pick it up, your chopsticks would form an X, and this is very impolite. When the food is so large that it makes the chopsticks form such an X, they say the eater is very greedy."

The ladies that knew Mu Lan were teasing her all the time about me, I could tell by the way they looked at us both. She never did stop blushing, and her sister was giggling every minute.

Like when we went to the Happy World, we sure had a wonderful time.

We left in a trishaw after a while, and it was pretty late. We had to travel down some dark streets, and a couple of times going around a corner I thought I heard a soft kind of noise; and then I had a funny feeling that somebody was following us.

I heard the noise again, and got the trishaw to turn another corner and then all of a sudden stop. And sure enough close to the houses I could see two men riding bicycles. And even in the moonlight I could see the bicycles were green.

But I didn't say a word to Mu Lan.

Chapter V

The bicycles come to the boat every day for a hour or so after that. And whenever I went out at night I always thought I heard them following. But we figured Fu Manchu was trying to scare us and make us pay the protection money, so we didn't pay any attention. I guess you get used to anything. After a while we kind of missed them when we didn't see any around.

Except for the bicycles everything kept on going fine at the school. When G.B. had bought the jukeboxes and the pin ball machines, the German fellow that sold them had thrown in what they call a tape recorder. And G.B. made recordings of some of his talks, especially the ones "How to Become a Millionaire," so he could go off with Alf once in a while fishing. And in case he didn't get back in time, it'd be the same as if he was around.

The students did better and better, especially Tak Thong, the little monk, and Gunga Das, the Hindu. They could both make speeches now would make your hair stand on end. And G.B. said he'd never seen anybody learn as fast as Tak Thong in the class how to make money. And then one night Tak came to the school all excited; and he told us how the abbot had got a kind of heart attack and had to quit, and the other monks had made him abbot instead.

Course he couldn't be around so much after that, he was busy at the temple. And we got a little worried about him when we heard the pigeons there had left all of a sudden and didn't come back. And a lot of the people in town got terrible scared, and said the volcano'd blow up or something. But the pigeons flew back in a week or so and everything was all right.

I was walking along the river with Mu Lan one afternoon, when I saw a big crowd on the bank. They were all looking at something and I looked, too, and I saw a man out in the water calling "Help! Help!" And then I saw his arms go up and he started to go under. But queer thing, not one of the people on the bank lifted a finger to save him. Even though there were plenty of fishermen around in their boats that could have pulled him up in a second.

"What's the matter?" I said to Mu Lan. "Ain't they going to help him?"

She asked a question of a old Chinese woman standing there, and then looked very sad. "O Tuan, they are afraid," she said. "The River God has taken him. They fear if they try to save him now the River God will take them also."

Well, course I couldn't see a poor fellow drown because of a foolish thing like that, so I jumped in, and swam out to get him. He'd gone down for the third time when I come up to him, and I pulled him onto my shoulders. And I made the shore, and laid him on the bank, and he sure looked like a goner. But I gave him what they call artificial respiration like I learned in the Army; and after a while he comes to, and sits up, and begins to cough the water out of him.

He's a pitiful fellow, maybe thirty, I guess, but his face is so squinched-up with worry and trouble he looks almost as old as Mock Duck. He's tall for a Chinaman and as skinny as a piece of hay standing in the field back home after a long dry spell; his arms and legs are like pieces of broken-off straw the same way. He's so weak and shaky it looks like a single puff of wind'd blow him over. He's all yellow, too, like the straw, yellower than most other Chinese, because even if he ain't old he's already bald, and his head's like a shiny, ripe pumpkin. With the water dropping off him everywhere he looks like a Chinese scarecrow that got worn out and somebody threw into the river.

The scarecrow body begins to shake, and the pumpkin head coughs out more water. And then he begins to sob like his heart'd break.

"O Tuan, it would have been better if you had let me drown," he says.

And then between sobbing and coughing he tells me how he's a trishaw driver and everything's gone wrong; and his wife and kids were getting hungrier and hungrier and he didn't have a penny. So he decided to kill himself and took a seat on his trishaw; and started pedaling as fast as he could and pedaled right into the river. And then when he got into the water, he changed his mind, and tried to save himself but couldn't. And now he was out he changed again and wished that he had died.

I told him to cheer up, how things were never as bad as they seemed and every cloud has a silver lining; I told him some of the sayings in the Wisdom of the World back of the dictionary and other sayings in the Success School like "Every Man a King," and things like that out of the book G.B. wrote. And it seemed like he listened and it did him good. And pretty soon I help him pull the trishaw out of the water and Mu Lan and me walk with him back to the boat.

He said his name was Wong Chu but everybody called him Teddy.

It looked to me like what he needed most was a good meal so I fed him some soup and ham and eggs and gave him a few dollars. And then I thought how we ought to help the people there every way we could, and here was a good chance. So I told him to come to the school, and I'd teach him how to get along in the world, and it wouldn't cost him a penny. And his pumpkin face lighted up like you'd turned on a electric bulb inside.

"You will be my guru, Tuan," he says. "You will be my guru that I will follow to the door of death."

"What's a guru?" I ask.

And he says it's a Hindu word meaning a teacher, that he will follow like a god.

He started coming to the classes next day and he follows me around like my shadow. And I never saw anybody learn as fast as he did in my life.

Well, another week passed and I didn't notice anything different with the green bicycles. So like before, we figured they were just waiting, trying to wear us down. A Dutchman I met told me the Chinese are the most patient people in the world. They'll put a lot of poison inside a young fruit tree maybe won't have fruit for twenty years, and then the fellow they're getting even with for taking their wife or something will eat the fruit and die, and nobody knows what killed him. And course they got the hundred-year-old eggs.

And then there was rumors of a new kind of trouble. We heard Tak was making a lot of changes over at the temple of the Sleeping Buddha; and some of the old Buddhist priests and the mullahs of the Malay churches and the witch doctors they call Bomos and the other old-timers didn't like it. And they didn't like what the school was doing other ways, and they were getting mad.

And then something else happened, too. All of a sudden things at the school began going bad. The students began dropping out fast, and no new ones were coming. Even the class How to Become a Millionaire didn't have hardly anybody now, and that was the most popular of all.

It kept getting worse and worse and looked like if something didn't happen pretty fast there wouldn't be anybody left except Tak Thong, when he could come, and Gunga Das and Teddy. And course Teddy wasn't paying.

"It's like I said," Bertie told us at the Four Elephants. "It's another of the bloomin' mysteries of this bloomin' East. In the morning you go out with your Chinese or Malay or Indian girl you been seeing for ten years and her voice is dripping honey. And that night she gives you chopped tiger whiskers in your rice that stick in the linings of your stomach like twenty packs of broken needles. And next morning you're dead and even in Heaven St. Peter can't tell you why she done it. . . . Alf, if you're going to let that drunk lay on the floor all day move him off to one side so he ain't right where people walk on him. Some of these Czech sailors got spikes in their shoes and I don't like blood on a nice, clean floor."

Then one morning the mail come from the States, and G.B. got some newspapers. And there was some pictures of one of them new colleges down in Florida or Hollywood somewheres starting a big radio Amateur Hour, like the time I went to Louisville, to teach them public speaking and theater and things. The men and the girl students were doing kind of vaudeville acts, playing guitars and saxophones, and then there were other pictures of them having a big dance.

G.B. is looking at the pictures when all of a sudden he gives a shout. "I got it!" he says. "We been giving 'em a

63

education all right, but we forgot about letting 'em have some fun. All work but no play ain't good for nobody. We'll have a radio Amateur Hour even if there ain't a radio station in Menang. People'll like that sure. And after that we'll give 'em a big dance. We'll have a real ball."

Well, we had the first party the next Thursday night. We put the microphone and the loudspeaker outside on the deck, and told the people what was going to happen. And in a little while half Menang was on the bank, waiting for the show to begin. And then the students began coming, bringing their friends, so many we had to put a rope on the doorway.

G.B. told the students to imagine they were going on a big radio station, and then the fun began.

I started things off by coming out dressed like a moonshiner, carrying a gun and a fruit jar of whisky, and I sang *The Hog-Eyed Man*, just like the time in Louisville. And then Mu Lan came out fixed up like a mountain girl, wearing a apron and a sunbonnet. And she looked cuter than ever. And she sang *On Top of Old Smoky* like I taught her. And then we sang it together. And everybody clapped so hard you'd have thought it was rocks falling from a quarry. And then G.B. did a German recitation, *Hans and Adolf at a Bull Fight*, and he acts out all the parts, even the bull and the horses. And after that he done a Irish one about Pat and Mike in their new automobile, and neither of them can drive. And the way he imitated the people yelling and honking and the police cars and the ambulances and the fire trucks coming, it was better than a ten dollar seat at a circus.

And then some Chinese students come out calling themselves the Menang Melody Five. There was only three of them, but they seen that Melody Five somewheres and thought it sounded nice. And they began playing that Chinese music is like a buzz saw cutting down a fence full of howling cats. And then a couple of Chinese girls, some of the ones that wore the glasses, walk out dressed like cowgirls in big hats and chaps made out of paper, and they sing *Git Along Little Dogie*. And then some of the Malay girls do the dancing like they're gold statues, while the Malay fellows beat the gongs.

And then all of a sudden the gong music stops, and G.B. pulls back a curtain. And there's a jukebox, what they call the Niagara box, has a picture of Niagara Falls lights up like a rainbow when it plays. I guess you know the Niagara; it's the best kind of jukebox there is. And it begins playing some fine dance music, and everybody starts doing jazz dances and the twist, just like they seen in the movies.

They sure went crazy over that American music and dancing. I guess because the Malay dancing is so slow.

When we seen how the party was such a big hit we had one every week. And all the students that were drifting away came back, and we had more than ever.

"We got to make the classes more interesting, too," says G.B. at breakfast after the first party. "I rode on the train once from St. Louis to Kansas City to see if I couldn't get my wife to stop that alimony. I been thinking about it this morning. There was a fellow opposite me was a big teacher, teaching handwriting or something in a big college. Right now he wasn't teaching; he was riding handcuffed to the sheriff, because he put the handwriting someway on other people's checks. We talked the whole trip, and it sure was interesting. He said the best teaching is when it's like playing. These people here like to play more than anybody in the world. And that's the way, whenever we can, we got to make the school in Menang."

So next thing for some of the lessons he has them say poems that he makes up—ain't anybody that don't like a good poem—and some he makes them sing like radio commercials.

We had got to be good friends with Bertie and Alf, and one Sunday we went to Alf's house for Sunday dinner. Alf had a fat little Australian wife and about six kids, and after we ate, the wife and the kids started playing a card game a war buddy of Alf's in the States had sent the kids for Christmas. It was a game named Pit they play back home where you pretend you're on the stock market; and you buy and sell stocks like you were rich, and were Andrew Carnegie and John D. Rockefeller fighting.

G.B.'s eyes all light up when he sees the kids playing. "That's a wonderful game," he says. "It's just what the horse doctor ordered. For my class on How to Be a Millionaire."

And he persuades Alf and his wife to let him have the cards, giving the kids a little money to keep them from making a fuss.

That card game was the biggest hit of all. The Chinese and Malays are terrible gamblers anyway, and this struck them just right. They brought big piles of what they call Bank of Hell money, that's the paper money they burn at funerals to buy people out of hell. And the second the How to Be a Millionaire class was ended, they'd start playing the game. And they'd yell like they were crazy, and hold up their fingers, and click the wooden adding machines they call a abacus so fast it made you dizzy. They'd have never stopped playing, but at midnight we always sent them home. We didn't want anything to happen with them and the fellows on the green bicycles.

That abacus is the fourth word in the A's and in the whole dictionary. The last word in the A's is *azure*, that's another name for blue. The last word in the dictionary is *zwieback*. That's a kind of cake.

I tell you the school was sure changing things in the town. I didn't notice it till Tak came for me one afternoon, and Teddy took us in the trishaw over to the temple. Tak was plenty different than the skinny little fellow afraid to open his mouth that come to the school the day of the opening. He was round and fat now, like the Congressman from Muleshoe, and he talked a blue streak. And when we came near the temple you wouldn't have known it was the same place. Before it'd been so quiet, like I said, when a fish jumped it sounded like thunder. Now he had a loudspeaker in the street right by the gate connected to the temple bells, and you could hear them half a mile away.

He'd taken off the big hats of the monks and put on ones with no brims at all hardly so when they went out to beg they could look down and see exactly how much rice or money they were getting. And he gave them a per cent on all they collected. Before, they'd had a sacred footprint of Buddha you could look at free. Now if you wanted to see it, you had to pay fifty cents. He doubled the price it cost to get married, and charged four times more for a funeral. He said dying was a lot more important to a Chinaman than marrying. You only died once, but wives was a dime a dozen.

I already told how the day we were at the temple with the cat they were having a little fair, and it was just about empty. This time the place was jammed so full of people you didn't have room to slap a mosquito. Tak had rented a jukebox and four pin ball machines from us, and there were long lines of Chinese and Malays waiting to play them. The machines were flashing and the bells were ringing all the time, and the jukebox wasn't quiet a second. Before it took them six months to carve one of the little Buddhas; now they were making them out of plaster, and they could turn out 200 a day.

"I have learned much wisdom in the school, Tuan," says Tak, patting his fat stomach. "Especially have I learned the money wisdom from Tuan G.B."

I saw all the pigeons cooing in the pigeon house, and told

him how we'd been worried about him when we heard they'd all flown away.

He looks to see that nobody's around, and then kind of winks at me. "We monks have been most kind to the pigeons, Tuan. And I thought it was time for the pigeons to do us a kindness in turn. There are certain berries in the jungle whose smell makes the pigeons very sick. I collected many of these berries and in the night spread them about the house where the pigeons dwell. In the morning all the pigeons were gone."

He tossed some crumbs of bread to a couple of the birds, stalking like sultans near him. "As you know it is a sign of great disaster when the pigeons leave, Tuan. For pigeons, who fly through the air, learn these matters faster than we humble humans. So many people were in terror, and they came from everywhere to bring sacrifices to the temple and so keep the evil away. Then when I thought they had sacrificed enough, I took the berries from their house, and the pigeons returned at once. The temple is now rich, Tuan."

Next week the fellow that ran the little theater at the Happy World where the Malay girls danced came with one of the students to the party on the boat. And he saw the big crowd there and what a fine time the people were having. And he said things hadn't been so good in the theater lately, and he figured maybe it'd help if he changed to our kind of dancing. And he said he'd try making it a taxi-dance place, like he'd seen in the movies. So he rented a big fancy jukebox from us, and when I met him a couple of weeks later he said he was doing a rushing business.

After that a couple of the teahouses that had the gong orchestras put in the jukeboxes, too. And we heard the old-timers were getting awful foolish now, and saying we were ruining the town. And that sure was a funny thing to say, when we were trying to make it better.

I stopped one afternoon at the Four Elephants, where a

Hindu snake charmer was sitting in the middle of the floor and playing a flute, hypnotizing a cobra in a basket.

Alf looks worried when he sees me and he talks kind of low, instead of roaring like a bull when you're putting a ring in his nose.

"You've got this town standing on its bloody ear, Oral," he says. "The Malay fellows that play the gongs are wild because they say the jukeboxes are taking their jobs. And the bloody monks in the other temples have seen what a fine life the ones in Tak Thong's place are having, and they're saying they want the same thing, so the old priests that run the temples are getting bloody apoplexy."

He gives the bar a swipe with a dirty rag. "For the bloody first time I been here the Malays and the Chinese and even the Hindus have got together. They been to see the Tunku's brother, too, and that means they'll be tied up with the Harmonious Daggers. I hear some of the old fellows are coming to see you tomorrow. You better get your bloody reception committee ready. . . . Frenchie, I told you once to quit teasing that cobra. People get bloody annoyed when you ask 'em to stop drinking to carry a dead man out of a bar."

Well, I went back right away and told G.B. what Alf said. But there wasn't much we could do, except be sure our guns were handy.

That night the Chinese on the green bicycles rode up after dark and stopped right by the gangplank, and they'd never done that before. And I woke up around maybe two or three o'clock, kind of restless, and looked out the window, and I could see they were still there.

The old-timers came just after breakfast, about twenty I guess, about half of them Malay, and half Chinese, and maybe a couple of Hindus. And most of them looked like they were straight out of a Chinese Bible, with long white hair and white beards.

We were terrible polite to them, and at first they were all right. Mu Lan brought them tea and betel nut, and they sat around and drank and chewed. Most of them couldn't talk English, being old-timers. But some of them could, particular the fellow that was the boss, a fat little Chinaman with a bald head and shiny round face, looked like one of those good luck Buddhas with fat naked stomachs I seen in the souvenir places in New Orleans you can buy for a dime.

He was dressed pretty fancy in a red silk robe all trimmed with silver and gold. He was the head priest of the big snake temple, they said, and that made him the highest priest in Menang, because the snake temple was the temple of the Tunku and his brother.

He was all smiling, like the good luck Buddhas now, and he looked like a pretty nice fellow. And G.B. and me talked to him about all kinds of things the way people do there before they get down to business; about whether the tigers was bad this year, and when the typhoons would be hitting the island. And you'd have thought he just came over for a little game of cards or checkers or maybe to pass the time of day.

And then everybody got quiet and all of a sudden it came; like back home on a beautiful summer day when you can't see a cloud in the sky there's a terrible clap of thunder.

"We are the elders of Menang," says the fat priest, still smiling. "And we have come to ask you for a little favor. We ask you to close the school."

Chapter VI

For the first time since I knowed G.B. for a minute he couldn't say a word. He was so surprised he just stood there kind of like Chang, the cat, did when he meowed after a bird he couldn't catch; his mouth kind of quivered but no sound came out.

Finally he manages to speak. "I don't think I'm hearing you right, Doc," he tells the priest. Everybody that was a big man G.B. always called Doc or Judge. "What was that you were saying?"

The priest smiles again. "We ask you to close the school, Tuan."

G.B. turns as red as the ace of diamonds on his cuff buttons. "You're in the wrong pew in the wrong church, Doc," he says.

71

The priest looks at him kind of wondering, and you can see he don't understand.

"What I mean is people in this town like our school," says G.B. "Times change, the way they say, Doc. And you got to change with the times."

The priest's face gets terrible hard. He stands there a minute thinking; his eyes look like one of the space men's eyes in the movies when they're getting ready to give somebody the death ray.

"We will see," he says all of a sudden, and he folds his red robe around his fat stomach, and walks down the gangplank slow and heavy, like he had on the space man's iron shoes. And the others follow him the same way.

As soon as they were out of sight, Teddy comes hurrying to me. His yellow scarecrow face and the skin on his yellow pumpkin head are drawn all tight with worry.

"O Tuan, there will be grave trouble now," he says. "Some of these men are high in the councils of the Harmonious Daggers. You saw the evil ones with their bicycles watching the boat last night. Now they will wait no longer; they will surely arrange an accident. I need the ears of a fox and the eyes of a hawk now, Tuan. I must never leave your side a moment."

This Teddy was really becoming wonderful. I thought Tak Thong and Gunga Das had been smart at the school, but they weren't nothing to Teddy. His mind worked so fast his head was like one of them ant circuses that have the ants in a little glass case so you can look right inside and see them milking their ant cows and everything; you could almost see Teddy's brains working. Funny thing, he was smiling and happy pretty near all the time now and he was feeding like a horse ain't eaten for half a year; but he stayed as skinny and like a Chinese scarecrow as ever.

It was only a few days when the accident he'd talked about came. I was walking with him and G.B. down a narrow street in the middle of town when all of a sudden a young Chinese comes racing along on a bicycle, riding like he was crazy.

"Look out!" shouts Teddy.

The bicycle would have hit us sure, but we both give a big jump like a couple of kangaroos. And we almost jumped right into a automobile coming the other way a mile a minute.

"Jump!" shouts Teddy again.

We missed that one, too, I don't know how. It was so close one of the door handles bruised G.B.'s arm and tore a big piece out of my coat. And a minute later we seen Fu Manchu walking along, and we knew just how it happened.

We get back to the boat and Teddy pins up the torn places in my coat just like he was a tailor.

"O Tuan, you and Tuan G.B. must be more careful now than ever," he says. "Because they have failed and they do not wish to lose face. They will not try to kill you as they would kill a Chinese. You are Americans and this would cause them much trouble. I think they will try to kill you with kuntaow."

"What's kuntaow?" I say.

And he tells me it's a Chinese thing like jujitsu and kurate, only it's so secret and so powerful it makes them two look like a kindergarten. He'd studied it for ten years, he said, from what they call a old master he met once riding in his trishaw. The old masters, he told me, could knock a man out just by blowing on him, even if he was ten feet away; and some of them could stop a tiger. Course I didn't believe it much, but like the detective from Scotland Yard in the Fu Manchu comic said, you never know what a Chinese can do.

Teddy said he'd take me that night to see a kind of beginning kuntaow. He thought maybe we'd like to put it in the school.

I get into his trishaw after supper and ride to a gloomy part of town where there ain't many people, and we see a little temple with a light burning inside.

"I will go and find out if they will let you in, Tuan," he says, and he leaves me there in the dark by myself. He's gone about half an hour and I'm beginning to get worried and then I see him coming back. He says he's sorry it took so long, but the temple people had to ask the god about me. And the god was awful slow deciding.

I went in with Teddy and there's the statue of the big god above the altar—you could tell right away he's the boss by the kind of sarcastic way he looks at all the little gods standing on each side of him and the fancy robe he's wearing.

Out in front of him there's a bunch of maybe fifteen young Chinese fellows and a couple of Chinese girls; and they're all in what you call a trance, with their bodies all stony and their eyes all glassy, like they were walking in their sleep. And they're swishing those big double swords like I seen once in a Jap movie around their heads, and throwing spears, and battle-axes, and swinging something I don't know the name of that's five or six pieces of lead pipe, tied together with chains, and is something like a cat-of-nine-tails, maybe seven feet long. Only it's made of lead and iron instead of leather; and it'll knock out your brains or tear out your insides if it just touches you. The young fellows and the girls are taking their orders from a priest in a black robe that's all glassy-eyed the same as them. And when they come near me and begin swinging those swords and chains so close to my head my hair waved with the wind, I sure didn't like it.

And then all of a sudden the glassy eyes of all of them kind of fade away, and the sleep walking stops, and they become regular people; and they're awful nice and serve me cakes and tea.

And Teddy tells the priest how I had a school, too, and he

kisses my hands and calls me brother. He said in his kuntaow school when you graduated, if you were attacked by
bandits and started fighting, you called on the school god.
And the god made six or maybe more people jump up to
your side looked exactly like you, and the bandits couldn't
tell which one was you and which were the spirits, so they
didn't know which one to hit. He wanted to know if he
could come over and teach at our school sometimes; but I
told him ours was a little different.

After we left I told Teddy it was the craziest thing I ever
heard of. But then I got to thinking about it, and I figured
maybe it was done with hypnotizing, like they say it is with
the Indian rope trick when the fellow throws up a rope and
a Hindu boy climbs it into the sky.

And then something happened that changed everything
and made me forget all about kuntaow and the accident
when they tried to kill us, and everything else.

The thing that made me forget was Rani.

She came with her mother one afternoon to join the
school, and after that nothing was ever the same. Her
mother was a little Hindu woman, round and fat as the coconut she was always eating and her father was a Malay and
she had some Dutch blood, too. And if you never seen anybody with them countries mixed up, you ain't ever seen a
pretty girl. She was tall and slender with long, golden hair
trailing down her back; she moved like a swan I seen once
on a lake at a zoo. Her head and her body were so delicate
shaped you were afraid to touch her hardly; you felt you
might break something, the way you do one of them fancy
statues in a museum that's worth a million dollars maybe.
Her skin was the color of her hair; when I see her first standing there it was like she was made out of gold.

She was wearing a beautiful embroidered sarong and a
wreath of yellow flowers in her hair. It made her look like
the queen of a island in the South Seas I saw once in the

pictures that half a dozen native fellows shot themselves for when she runs off with a sailor.

But it was her eyes that were so wonderful. They were big and kind of golden brown and shone with a beautiful light. When you looked into them you felt you were floating off somewhere in a kind of jungle maybe full of wild orange trees and colored birds and strange flowers that put you to sleep with their perfume. Or maybe you were out on Mars or someplace with the space people and you didn't ever want to come back.

She was the most beautiful girl I ever saw in my life.

She'd just started working as a dancer at the Happy World, she said, and she'd heard about the school and came. She liked Western ways, and she wanted to become a Western girl, and maybe, I guess, marry a Western man.

Well, I'd heard plenty of times about love at first sight, and I never believed it. But that afternoon when I met Rani, I knew it was true. It was like . . . like you was standing by a swimming pool talking to Mu Lan, and G.B. and some other people were standing there, too. And then Rani came along, and just that second somebody behind you hit you over the head with a sledge-hammer and knocked you into the water. And you were under a long time, seemed like a hundred years maybe. And then you came up again and all the people at the pool and everywhere in the world were gone; there wasn't anybody left but Rani. And wherever you went after that, and wherever you looked, at the ocean or up in the sky, all you could see was a thousand Ranis with the wreath of flowers in her hair, and maybe her fat little mother eating coconut. I fell head over heels in love the first minute.

I didn't want to really. I was terrible fond of Mu Lan, and even though to me we was just wonderful friends, I kind of thought maybe with her it was different, and I knew it'd make her feel sad. I hate to hurt anybody, and I'd have done almost anything to keep from hurting somebody meant as much to me as Mu Lan. But I couldn't any more have stopped falling in love with Rani than the engineer on a hundred-car freight could have stopped a train going sixty miles an hour down one of those big mountains back of Chattanooga, when all of the brakes was burned out.

Well, she signed up for the school and I stayed with her every minute I could spare. And whenever I could after the school finished at night I went out to the dance place at the Happy World where she worked. One night a week she did the Malay dances with the gongs, and six nights it was the taxi dances. I sure didn't like that taxi dancing; but she and her mother needed the money. And it wasn't like some of the places in the East where the girls pick up any man they see; all the Malay and Chinese girls here were terrible strict, and Rani's mother and the mothers of the other girls were with them every minute. Fact is, people said the mothers brought their daughters there so they'd meet some rich Malay or Chinese and that way make a good marriage.

I ain't any good at dancing, so I'd buy a bunch of tickets and sit with Rani and her mother and just talk.

I stop with G.B. at the Four Elephants as usual for a beer, and Bertie looks different. And then I see he's got a box he's standing on behind the bar to make him look taller.

"You better watch yourself, Oral," he says. "You ain't just girl crazy, that's all right. But you're marriage crazy, that's wrote all over you. A bloomin' Malay girl's fine, and a bloomin' Hindu girl's fine, too. But when you marry one that's a bloomin' half and half it's like powdering yourself with TNT and then playing with matches."

"Best thing is play with them all, but marry none," says G.B., sinking his round face in a big mug of beer. "They'll all cheat the living daylight out of you. I married three times, women I got out of the 'Lonely Hearts Guide,' that was all guaranteed, and each of 'em swore when they sent

77

their pictures they had over fifty thousand. The first one said she had a house and fifty thousand, and after I married her I seen the house. It was one of them houses made out of fifty thousand toothpicks. And the second one had fifty thousand bees that'd sting the life out of you if you tried to get a spoonful of honey without telling her. The third one had fifty thousand used four-cent stamps. That's the one I'm paying the alimony to in Kansas City. Course I didn't marry 'em for their money. But you sure like people to keep their word."

"Like Bertie says, anyway don't get mixed up marrying one of them bloody half and halfs," grumbles Alf. "I knowed a half-Hindu, half-English girl I met in a bloody dance hall in Singapore. And I bought her a couple of beers and was dancing around with her, nice and gentlemanly, when all of a sudden I see the head of a bloody little cobra come out of the neck of her dress, and the little devil starts spitting at me. Course I let her go like a shot, but she says 'Don't be scared, dearie. That's only George. He's just woke up, and he's always a little jumpy then. I ain't got a mother like the other girls here to take care of me. So he lives inside my dress just in case people get fresh.' "

Mu Lan didn't say anything to me about Rani. She brought some little present for the boat every day like she'd always done, a funny little Chinese clown that dances on a string or a puzzle made of pieces of wood you couldn't put together in a hundred years; but you hardly ever heard her soft little laugh like the ice tinkling in the creek. And she never did play the pretty little game, opening and shutting the fan and hiding her face anymore.

I was sitting with Rani and her mother in the Happy World one night, watching the other girls dancing, when a Malay fellow come in dressed up fit to kill, looks as rich as John D. Rockefeller. Most of his clothes are like people wear in the States; you couldn't tell any difference. But he's got a half dozen rings on his fingers shining with diamonds and rubies big as baseballs pretty near; and he's got a sarong looks like it's solid gold tied around his waist.

And there's two fellows with him dressed the same way, except they haven't the rings and their sarongs are just plain green silk. Everybody when the gold sarong comes near stands up and gives a kind of nervous bow; and some soldiers standing around click their heels and salute.

He comes closer now and I see him plainer. He's a big fellow, kind of puffy, with tricky kind of eyes like a fox; he reminded me of the fellow run a lunch stand in Muleshoe that if you didn't watch him'd give you a hamburger wasn't nothing but fat.

"It is the Tunku's brother, Tuan," says Rani, her big eyes looking kind of scared, like when a deer sees a hunter. "I think he has come tonight to pick a new girl."

And she kind of draws back away from the floor, so she won't be noticed so easy.

Pretty soon the Tunku's brother comes down the line of girls with the two green sarongs walking slow behind him, and looks each one over careful. He comes to Rani, and stops a minute and another minute, and I think sure there's going to be trouble. But he walks on again to the end of the line, and I figure now everything will be all right. And then in a minute one of the green sarongs comes hurrying back; and he taps Rani on the shoulder and says something to her in Malay. And she answers so low I can hardly hear and points to the tickets I'm holding.

She turns to me and her voice is all shaky. "The Tunku's brother wishes to dance with me, Tuan," she says.

I look at her, sort of asking what she wants to do, and she nods her head, meaning she'd better try it. So even if I have the tickets for the whole evening, I figure since he's the Tunku's brother it's polite to let him have one dance.

79

So the green sarong bows to me and takes her off to his boss; and the jukebox begins playing a jazz tune and Rani and the Tunku's brother move out on the floor and start dancing. I watch them close but he's acting all right, talking fast, and smiling a oily smile, the way the lunch stand fellow used to do when he was dishing you out stale pork chops.

And then the music stops. And I wait for the green sarong to bring her back but there's no sign of him coming. I can see Rani's getting more nervous, but she kind of signals me not to interfere, and I think all right, I'll let him have one more number. And the music starts and the Tunku's brother dances with her again, and I see it's a kind of twist. And then the music ends, and I wait again but the green sarong doesn't bring her back this time either. I'm getting mad now, so I walk over to where the Tunku's brother's sitting with her. And I can see by the way she's edging off from him she doesn't want to dance with him any more. And then I see he's pretty drunk.

So I turn to the green sarong fellow and pull out my tickets.

"The lady's engaged all the evening," I say, talking kind of haughty like the lady that was a foreman at the cotton mill in Atlanta when she was getting ready to fire one of the girls.

The green sarong flicks a ash from his cigarette so it falls on my coat, but I can't be sure whether or not it's a accident. "It's the Tunku's brother who wishes the dance," he says, each word like that dry ice, so cold it burns you.

I move a couple of steps forward so I can take Rani away.

"I'm sorry, I don't speak Malay," I say, awful sarcastic. "What's a Tunku? Is that the broiled meat you eat on a stick?"

"That's *sate*," he says blocking my path. "A Tunku's a

prince, a king. This is his brother. And I am the brother's aide."

I see the Tunku's brother trying to move closer to Rani, and my blood gets to boiling. I take a couple of steps toward her again.

"Pardon my ignorance," I say, looking at the fancy gold sarong the Tunku's brother is wearing. "I thought you was the tumbling act opening up a circus."

And then in a second the two green sarongs are on me, and I see their krisses flashing. I don't know what would have happened, but just that second a half dozen American sailors come in, and the Tunku's brother even if he's drunk knows they're worse than leopards just stepped in a nest of fire ants. So he calls to the others and they let me go. And I take Rani shivering, back to where her mother's waiting, and sit there, breathing hard. Pretty soon the Tunku's brother picks out another girl and starts whirling her around the floor. And Rani and me sit out another dance, and then I walk with her and her mother to the gate where Teddy's waiting with the trishaw.

We take them home, and on the way back to the boat I tell Teddy what happened.

His scarecrow eyes get tears in them now; he looks at me kind of like a father in the movies talking to his son that's going to be electrocuted.

"O Tuan! Do you not have enough enemies with the priests and the mullahs and the Harmonious Daggers without making an enemy of the Tunku's brother?" he moans. "What is this Rani but a girl you will forget tomorrow? Now I must watch over you doubly, Tuan. Like a mother watches her baby in a hammock in the jungle when there is a prowling tiger."

A few days later I went uptown and stopped a minute to watch a procession—they were always having some kind of

81

parade for a wedding or a funeral or a holiday. The street was terrible crowded with pushcarts and bicycles and donkeys, like every day, and people were always bumping into you, trying to get by. And then a little Chinaman in blue overalls comes along carrying a couple of buckets of hot shrimps over his shoulders, and somebody behind gives him a shove, and knocks him right into me. He puts a hand up to keep the shrimps from spilling out; and he hits me pretty hard and he's terrible apologetic.

"O Tuan, excuse please," he says, talking what they call pidgin English. "Many people in street. Push, push. Push him too much. Velly solly, Tuan."

And I tell him it's nothing. And course I forgot it right away.

And then next day I'm eating lunch when G.B. suddenly puts down the hamburger he's eating.

"What's the matter with you, Oral?" he says. "You're white as a angel's wings on wash day."

Course G.B. was always talking funny that way.

"I'm fine," I answer. "I ain't ever felt better."

And then it seems like all of a sudden the air's full of big fiery suns all whirling around like a Fourth of July gone crazy. And the next minute the suns burn out and I'm laying pretty near unconscious on the floor.

Well, course G.B. rushes to pick me up; and Mu Lan and Mock Duck and Teddy come running out the kitchen to see what's the matter.

And G.B. gets the Dutch doctor that's there, and he can't see anything wrong. And he gives me some pills for indigestion, and says take them four times a day, and drink plenty of water, and then he goes away. I keep getting worse and worse, and then that night Teddy gets suspicious. And he begins asking questions about what I done—I told you he was terrible smart. And pretty soon I remember about the fellow bumping into me and hitting me in the chest.

And then I remember thinking afterward maybe I saw the fellow looks like Fu Manchu going off in the crowd.

And then the yellow in Teddy's scarecrow face and bald head turns kind of deathly white, like you dusted a yellow cushion with chalk. And he says, "It's kuntaow." And this time he really starts crying and I can see he thinks I'm going to die. And he says terrible things about himself, because he left me alone for even a minute. And then I go almost unconscious again. And I hear Teddy saying to G.B. like in a dream, that there's only one thing that can save me now, a master of kuntaow. And if they don't get one quick, in the morning I'll be dead.

Next thing I know they're rushing me off in the trishaw. And they take me to a little house on a dark street, and a Chinaman is there wearing a blue skullcap and blue gown and has a white beard reaches pretty near to his waist. I see his blue skullcap leaning over me, and I can tell he's looking at my chest to find out if there's any marks. But he's all hazy, like when G.B. and me were on the towboat on the river and there was a heavy fog.

And then he kind of wakes me from my dream and asks me a couple of questions; and his voice sounds like it's a ghost talking.

"Do you know the minute and the hour when this Chinese carrying the shrimp bucket struck you, Tuan? It is very important, Tuan."

The suns in my head now are like a lot of steam rollers going crazy in a road, but I manage to make them stop.

"It was ten minutes after two," I say, like I was talking to him through water. "I'd just looked at my watch."

"Did he strike you with one or two fingers, Tuan?"

"It was two fingers," I say.

And then the steam rollers start again. But I can hear him and G.B. whispering, and it's like two ghosts talking.

"It is what we call the circulation method of kuntaow,"

the old man says to G.B. "There is in the body a vital point in the blood, which moves about according to the different times of day. We who know kuntaow know how to touch this point. And if we do this in a certain way the person we so touch may as well step into his coffin. . . . I do not know if I can save your friend. But perhaps the gods will be kind."

He takes some different kinds of drugs from a lot of bottles he has on shelves, and mixes up some terrible smelling kind of drink, and pours it down my throat. And then G.B. and Teddy carry me out to the trishaw again, and take me back to the boat.

Well, for four days I lay there, with everybody around me like ghosts now. It was like a comic they had where all the people was ghosts, but they come back to the earth once in a while. It was a good comic.

I guess G.B. and all the rest of them thought I was as good as dead. Mu Lan was there pretty near every minute, nursing me, and Rani came, too, whenever she didn't have to be dancing. And course Teddy and Mock Duck and Amok, and G.B. whenever he could get away from what he had to do for the school. And sometimes when they were in the room I could see their lips moving, and I knew they were praying. Even G.B., and I never seen him do that before.

Mu Lan was a wonderful nurse. She'd sit for hours by the bed, giving me the medicine from the kuntaow doctor, and making me bird's nest soup and things, trying to get me to eat because I didn't have any appetite. She was like the way she used to be before I met Rani, all happy and laughing the soft laugh like the ice again. And she'd draw pictures for me and tell me all kinds of Chinese stories, about how there was a woman lived in the stilt house next to her had a beard a foot long, and they said she got that way from eating tiger meat. And sometimes she'd sing *On Top of Old Smoky*.

And then I'd start to teach her *Blue Fly* maybe—that's a fine mountain song—and in the middle everything'd kind of fade and I'd drift off and wouldn't know whether I was in Menang or singing down at Louisville for the Amateur Hour. Then I'd wake up, and I'd see her sitting there, fixing something for me with her tiny hands, just like a doll.

And then Rani'd come in with her mother for a few minutes before she had to go to work, and Mu Lan's face'd get all sad and she'd leave. And Rani'd sit down by me, and Mu Lan and everything else'd be wiped out, like when you cleaned the blackboard in school with the eraser. Rani believed in the Hindu religion, and she'd talk to me about what they call reincarnation, and how maybe we'd met before when we was a couple of ants. And then she'd sing a Hindu love song, and it was so soft and sad it broke your heart pretty near.

Once I had a splitting headache and her mother went out of the room for a minute, and Rani leaned over and began stroking my forehead. And it was kind of like she was singing the song again, only this time through her fingers. And it felt wonderful, and pretty soon all the trouble in my head and everywhere in the world was gone.

And then her mother came in all of a sudden and seen her doing it, and gave her a awful scolding, because the Hindu girls ain't supposed to even see a man unless they're married, and course touching him is terrible.

Once I saw the Kitchen God wasn't in his usual place but was out on the deck with the sun beating down so hot it was blistering the paint on him. And Mock Duck was sitting by him, like a cross old raccoon, watching to see how he was taking it. A couple of hours later, it was pouring rain and coming down big chunks of hail, and Mock Duck was still out there with the god, watching the same way. He came inside when the weather got too bad, but he left the god out in the storm. And when I asked him what he was doing, he said he was punishing the god for not looking after me better.

Well, on the fifth day I was sitting up, and the sixth day I'm still pretty weak but it was almost like nothing had happened. And Teddy takes me out in the trishaw along the river to get some air. Mu Lan's sitting by me, fanning me with a big paper fan, because it's terrible hot and the flies and the gnats are bad. Rani couldn't be there; they were having a special dance for a big bunch of tourists just off a cruise boat.

Some young Chinamen go past riding bicycles. They ain't gangsters, just young fellows having a good time; but I guess it makes Teddy think of the others.

He stops the trishaw with a jerk, and turns round to talk to me. His yellow face and head are the deathly white again; he looks like a pumpkin splashed with whitewash. "I have learned who did this to you, Tuan. It is the Harmonious Daggers. They have done it for the priests and the mullahs and the Tunku's brother. They say they will not stop until they have put you in your grave."

I see the fan in Mu Lan's hand kind of quiver.

And I think about her and Rani. And I sure feel bad.

Chapter VII

Well, nothing happened to me for a while after that, and I figured they were just waiting so it'd be easier to catch me off guard. All the time we were getting more and more students. And they all worked terrible hard and studied until late at night. The lights on the boat was always the last thing in town to go out.

One time they were playing Pit and a snake come in off the wharf, to get out of the rain, I guess. And funny thing it was a krait, that was the snake where I stopped the first time reading the dictionary.

The two best students now were Gunga Das and Teddy. Whenever you'd see a crowd in the school you could figure it was Gunga Das making a speech. He'd have everybody hypnotized, like the Congressman at Muleshoe that talked once eighteen hours without stopping for what they called a Talkathon; and you couldn't take your eyes or ears off him. They had a fellow once in the drugstore window played the piano the same way, and he played twenty-seven hours without stopping. The piece he played most was *Mavourneen, Mavourneen*. That's a piece wrote about Ireland. The fellow played the piano was a German named Schmidt but they called him Smitty.

Gunga Das was talking about starting a political party against the Tunku's brother—they didn't have any kind of politics there because the Tunku's brother ran everything. But we told him to go easy. We didn't want him to get into any kind of trouble. Because when you got into trouble there, you generally always was shot.

The part of the school people liked the best, same as before, was when G.B. told them how to get rich. The room was so packed when he talked sometimes he had to give the speeches twice in a night to take care of everybody. But there were a couple of things happening made me think maybe the people wasn't understanding what we were teaching in the school just right, and I began to get kind of worried.

There were two little Hindu brothers when they came to the school were the meekest fellows you ever saw. They wouldn't have talked back to a stone rabbit; they'd be afraid he'd chase them. They were working for a Chinaman, copying the drawings on the walls of the temples, and the Chinaman sold them to the tourists that come off the boats for a quarter. They wanted to be big artists, they said, but like most of the others, they didn't have no confidence. But after being in the school a while, they'd spit in the eye of a tiger.

Well, one night they didn't come to the class, and I wondered why, because they never missed and they'd been working sometimes till after almost everybody had gone home. And next morning a lieutenant of the police come, a tall fellow with a black moustache so big you could have juggled baseballs on the points, and a couple of policemen were behind him.

"Where's Jinnah and Saddu?" he asks.

"I don't know," I say. "They were here a couple of nights ago. And they stayed like they always do after the class, making some kind of drawings."

"I know they've been making drawings," the lieutenant snaps. "They just did some drawings on a metal plate and made $100,000 in counterfeit money."

You could have knocked me over with a daisy petal.

"One good thing," says the lieutenant. "The counterfeits are easy to tell. They're better made than the original money."

We had a old Chinaman named Charley Wu was studying at the school, a nice gray-bearded fellow more scared even than Jinnah and Saddu when he started. He wanted to be a big gardener, he said, fixing up fancy plants and things for the rich Chinese in Menang; but like the others he'd never got anywhere because he didn't have any confidence neither. The minute he touched a plant he'd do everything wrong. But soon as he was at the school for a while it was like the difference between day and night. He had the deck of the boat covered everywhere with big boxes of flowers and plants growing ten feet high; he had the boxes even on the wharf, making a path of flowers leading to the gangplank like they have in front of fancy hotels. Whenever you seen him now he had a spade or something in his hand; he never got tired of digging and raking. He'd have stayed twenty-four hours a day if we'd let him.

Well, a few days after the business about the two Hindus, the police lieutenant came on the boat again.

"When did you see Charley Wu last?" he says, kind of grim.

"Two days ago," I say. "He was trimming up that big hedge of rosebushes."

"Let's chop down those rosebushes," says the lieutenant, and the police with him take a couple of big knives they're carrying and chop out the rosebushes fast. And behind them I see some flowers with beautiful red blossoms.

"Take a look," says the lieutenant, kind of nasty now.

"What are they?" I say. I'd never seen flowers just like that before.

"They're poppies," he says. "Charley Wu's been growing opium."

And he cuts down the other boxes, and they were all the same way.

About the same time an Englishman that managed a big rubber plantation on the island came in and said he'd heard about the school. And he was short-handed, he said, and he could use some of the students. So we sent him some of the best of them, specially those who'd been taking G.B.'s course about money. The English fellow come back in a week and I thought it was to thank us for sending such fine workers. But I was sure surprised when he said he'd come to ask us please not to send him any more.

"I've had to fire 'em all," he says. "Every blasted chappie in the lot. In the week I've had 'em they've stolen more rubber than I knew I had on the plantation. By Jove, they were clever. And Menang's jolly famous all through the islands for its honesty. I've been here thirty years, and I've never heard of a single blighter stealing a penny before."

I talked to G.B. about it, and how maybe we ought to slow them down a little and be sure they was on the right track. But he said wasn't anything to worry about. He said the big college fellow that he traveled with that time handcuffed to the sheriff said in any school you were bound to get maybe ten per cent that misunderstood and done the wrong thing; and you couldn't stop teaching all the good ones, just because of a few that was bad. And he said the fellow told him besides it was better to let them go too far in the beginning, and you could always pull them back, where if they never got started it was zero.

Well, G.B. kept thinking and thinking and improving the school every minute. He made each student bring what they call a inspiring message each week, and read it out to the class; you know like "There's a path up the highest mountain" and "Hitch your wagon to a star." They helped the people plenty. And some of them sure made you think.

The Chinese are awful good at those kind of sayings. I guess you seen them on the Chinese fortune cookies. There was a Chinese restaurant near the filling station in Memphis had the best fortune cookies anywhere. Some of the sayings in them'd make you bust your sides laughing, like "Don't open your mouth too wide, you dope. You'll put your foot in it." G.B. got plenty of his jokes, he told me, from the fortune cookies in that restaurant.

"Another thing I got to do is paint us up a good sign like a billboard," says G.B. "Before I knowed you I went around helping a carnival fellow was a wonderful painter, like the man you talk about painted the pictures to fit the frames. Anything you wanted this fellow could paint you a picture of in half a minute, a pretty girl, or a cow or a horse, or all of 'em put together. And he painted pictures in invisible ink, too, you couldn't see till you held 'em up to a fire. In between he painted houses and barns. I figure a good sign'll help us plenty."

And right away he painted a couple of big pictures and he put them together on the wharf by the boat. One of them showed a man dressed kind of shabby, standing all alone at a party, with his mouth hanging way down, like he had stomach trouble, and the other of a man dressed to kill, and talking and laughing with a lot of pretty Malay and Chinese girls crowding around him, all fighting to give him fancy things to eat and asking him for a dance. And there was a sign underneath the gloomy fellow, "This man stayed home," and a sign under the laughing one, "This man went to the Menang Success School." And then there was a big sign over both with a big question mark, "Which man would you rather be?"

We were in the big room working a day or so after when I hear somebody walking up the plank. He comes through the door and I'm surprised to see he's a American. He's a old man, dressed in a double-breasted black suit, like he's going to a wedding. It's pressed awful neat, and he has a handkerchief tucked in the pocket of his coat like the big society people; and in the lapel he's wearing a white flower. His hat is one of them stiff-brimmed black hats, looks like it's a hundred years old, and his hair under it is white as snow; he's got a white moustache that swings out from his face like the old cavalry sabers my grandfather had on the wall back in his cabin at Muleshoe. He looks exactly like one of those old fellows I seen in the movies that owned a big plantation in the Civil War.

I start to shake hands with him and the way he kind of hesitates I can see he's terrible shy.

"My name is Bascom," he says. "Calhoun T. Bascom. You may have heard my family name, though not of course of me. The family is well known in New Orleans. My sister was the queen of the Mardi Gras in 1913."

We tell him we stopped there on the towboat and his moustaches kind of light up. "I have been here since shortly after the second Great War," he says. "I came to escape the atomic bomb. Though I have found the latter judgment to be not well considered. As you know this is the area the nations have chosen to carry out their testing."

He straightens the handkerchief in his coat that was twisted a little to the side. "I taught for forty years in Miss Fairlee's School for Girls. This was one of the most fashionable schools in New Orleans. It was noted for the charm of its graduates. I taught deportment, and manners, and elocution, and also dancing and singing. It was said my voice was not ill-sounding. I saw your sign and I thought you might need a teacher to give some extra instruction."

G.B. looks at him, trying to figure him out. "We don't need nobody right now, Cal," he says, and when he said Cal, I saw the old man kind of wince. "It ain't exactly that kind of school." G.B. gives me a big wink. "You leave your address and if anything turns up we'll come and find you."

The old man looks awful disappointed. "I am sorry," he says. "The inflation in America keeps continuing, and the shrinkage in my income has been most serious . . . in fact, I will confess . . . it has been . . . devastating."

He stands there hesitating a minute, and a big ugly spider comes crawling over the floor. And he kind of shivers again, and pulls out a can of insecticide from a back pocket and takes careful aim, and squirts it at the spider. The spider runs off down a crack, and the old man shakes his head.

"It is a beautiful country here," he says. "But the insects are a galling burden. I am grateful for these insecticides. They are costly and require money I can ill afford. But without them my life would not be possible."

He squirts more of the spray down into the crack, and his face gets more worried. "I dread the day. But if my income shrinks so that I can buy the insecticides no longer, I will have to leave Menang."

And he tells us where he lives, and thanks us, and goes down the plank.

I felt kind of worried about him being a American way out there without any money, and I'd have liked to give him a job. But G.B. said we couldn't afford it.

We were in Bertie's place late that afternoon for our usual drink when a kid outside started flying a kite.

"Kite time's coming up," rumbles Alf, looking at him a

minute, then turning to watch a lady moving closer and closer to a big Dutch sailor that's asleep at the bar. "They'll be having the kite festival next month and the bloody kites are more important to 'em than women. Sometimes they have fights between teams from the different temples and things and they take 'em more serious than getting married. They put powdered glass on the bloody strings and then saw away at the other fellow's kite till the string cuts through and the one that don't fall down is the champion. . . . Miss, please drink your beer nice and quiet, will you? It ain't etiquette here for a lady to pick a bloody gent's pocket."

G.B.'s eyes give a sudden flash, like when you strike a match in the dark. And he starts pacing up and down, the way he does when he's excited. "I got a fine idea," he says. "It's about the school and the kite flying. Looks to me we ought to get up one of them teams and maybe fight the Buddhist temple down the wharf. It'll be a fine ad for the school."

Like I said, you could always figure on G.B.'s thinking up something smart. "That's sure right," I put in. "A old fellow that used to come to the filling station at Memphis sold pop at the big ball park. And he said all the big people out there told him there ain't anything in the world to beat athletics for good advertising."

So G.B. and me fix it up with the temple quick—I guess they figured they'd win easy because they were the best kite-flyers in town. And we knew Teddy was a pretty good flyer, so we made him the captain of the team.

Teddy had three other fellows with him from the school, a couple of Malays and a Hindu; and they got their kites all ready. They bought the powdered glass at the temple, because it had to be a special kind, blessed by the priest, and couldn't have any sharp pieces; and then they glued it to the strings and went out along the river practicing. They were wonderful kites they call moon kites, with half a dozen different shaped moons one under the other; they had a strip of grass tied tight on the back so when they were up in the air they buzzed like 10,000 hornets.

Well, I tell you that kite fight sure caused plenty of excitement. Every day you could see the temple team, three little Chinese monks and a little priest almost a dwarf that's the captain like Teddy, trying out different kinds of kites and racing down the river. And Teddy and our team was doing the same. And everybody in town was talking about it, and people were putting up all kinds of money. If they didn't know about the school before, they sure knew about it now.

And then the day of the festival comes; and the people betting and everybody else pretty near go crazy. We all hurry down to a big open place by the river where the fight's going to be, and you never saw so many kite flyers and so many kites in your life. Thousands of people, I guess, men and children and a few women, too; and everybody was pulling strings and running and yelling and grunting, almost breaking their necks trying to look up at the sky.

Some of the kites were made like cats and dogs and some like snakes and dragons, and some were fixed up like hawks and storks, and some like elephants and tigers.

And then our team comes out, the two Malays and the Hindu carrying small moon kites, and Teddy carrying the main one that's just one full moon painted all gold and is big as a house pretty near.

"You got to win this for us, Teddy," says G.B. "It means plenty to the school."

And Teddy just smiles a worried kind of smile, and tests the string to see if it's all right.

And then the four fellows come from the temple, the three little Chinese monks carrying the small moon kites like ours, and the little priest like a dwarf carrying the main one, that's a full moon almost twice as big as ours with a scary devil-face in the middle, painted black and red.

The other people pull down their kites now so they won't be in the way. And everybody starts talking at once, and you see the rich Chinese and Malays betting big handfuls of money. There was more excitement than when the *Natchez* raced the *Robert E. Lee*.

G.B. turns to a couple of kids standing there holding a kite different than any of the others.

"Up!" he says.

And the kids start running and get the kite up in the air fast. It's a big kite, has what they call a triple trailer hanging from it by some cords. The top of the trailer is a long canvas streamer, *Menang Success School,* and under that is a streamer *Develop Your Personality,* and under that *Every Man A King.* And after it's up a few minutes, G.B. turns to the kids again.

"Down!" he says.

And the kids pull it back to the ground.

And then all the people stop talking, and it gets quiet as a tomb.

And then the first of the temple monks runs out and gets his kite up high; and the first of our team does the same, and then the fight begins.

The kites start jumping and dodging like a couple of prize fighters in the ring; and they hum and buzz when they sweep down like they were giant bees. And the people everywhere begin yelling and betting like crazy again. And pretty soon the strings are touching, and they begin sawing back and forth. I'd seen the fights a couple of times before, and generally it took a long time, sometimes maybe a hour or so before a fight was ended. But today it was different. Teddy'd trained his people so good the string on our kite had just about touched the string on the temple fellows' when it cut through and the temple kite came tumbling down like a bomber that was hit in the war.

Course a big cheer went up from our crowd, and the temple monks looked awful gloomy, and the people that bet on them were awful mad. And then the second kites go up and the people get all excited again, and bet and yell some more. And our side wins a second time, and the third time it's the same way.

And the school crowd laughs and smiles, and the crowd from the temple grumbles, and some of them put their hands on their knives.

And then the little dwarf priest looks terrible solemn and picks up the big moon; and he looks at it everywhere, bottom and top, to see that the joints are all right. And then he takes a chew of betel nut and counts some holy beads around his neck; and then he bows his head and he kind of sings something you know is praying. And he holds the kite up in the air and lets out the string; and then he starts running like lightning. And a second later Teddy is doing the same.

This time the kites screech and scream and squeal and moan, just like they're alive. They whip up in the air, and swing and swoop, and climb and dive, like a couple of eagles battling. And after a few minutes they straighten out and then they meet head on. It looks like the temple kite is sure going to smash the school kite, because like I said it's almost two times bigger. And then the strings cross, and Teddy begins pulling like he's caught a whale. And then a terrible moan goes up from the temple crowd; and I see the temple kite falling, easy this time, like a fellow jumped out of the bomber and was floating down in a parachute. And the people from the school cheer like a bunch of lions roaring. And the fight's over.

And G.B. tells the kids to run up the kite with the Success School sign on it again, and everybody goes home.

On the way back I tell Teddy how smart he is to win so quick.

"O Tuan, it is what I have learned in the school," he says. "Without the school I would be nothing."

He looks around to see if anybody's watching, and shows me the string of his kite, and I can see little pieces of metal shining everywhere. "I broke them with a hammer," he says. "They are pieces of your old razor blades, Tuan."

Course I told him it was a terrible thing to do, and that wasn't what we were teaching in the school at all.

I wanted to tell the old priest what happened, but Teddy said they'd kill him if I did. So I couldn't say anything. And Teddy told me he was sorry, and wouldn't do it any more. I've thought about it plenty of times, and it bothers me yet. But I guess you can't make people perfect.

Next afternoon I was at Bertie's and Alf looked awful nervous.

"It's too bloody bad you didn't lose instead of winning, Oral," he says. "I was talking to some of the Chinese this morning and they say it's caused things with you and the bloody priests to be worse than ever. It's made the priests and the temple lose terrible face and losing face is the one thing here that drives people crazy. Like Bertie told you beating somebody in a bloody kite fight is worse than if you stole one of their women. If I were you I'd put some electric fences around the boat, and get a couple of them Great Dane dogs, like the bloody rich people. . . . Dutchie, don't let that drunk with the false teeth bite you that way. They say a bite from false teeth's poison as a bloody cobra."

A few days later I'm walking along the wharves with G.B. where they're putting up a big rubber warehouse. And just as we pass, a fellow carrying bricks on the second floor slips and dumps the whole load on us. I got a little knock from a brick on the shoulder, and another brick cracked the toe of G.B.'s right shoe. Neither of them was anything, but a couple of inches closer and we'd have both been dead. And something close as that sure gives you a scare.

And right after that I found a big scorpion in my bed, and the scorpions there ain't pretty.

A few days later I got a terrible headache again, with my head like you were blowing up a balloon too hard and it was getting ready to burst. And Teddy thought it was somebody doing the kuntaow again, and he brought the kuntaow doctor in a hurry. And the doctor didn't think it was any new kuntaow, but it might be the old one coming back. And he counted the days since the fellow with the shrimps hit me, and divided the number by seven. Because he said that the kuntaow fellows like to work in sevens, and they could hurt people this way up to seventy-seven days.

The number didn't come out exactly right, and he couldn't be sure whether it was the old kuntaow or some regular kind of sickness so he said anyway he'd better give me what they call acapuncture. He got Mu Lan to help him, because she was wonderful with a doctor, bringing him hot water and towels and things, and he stuck my head all full of needles, maybe a couple of hundred. And each one he put in, you could see in Mu Lan's doll face it was like he was putting them in her heart, though it didn't hurt me at all. And then he left the needles in my head and went away. And I guess I looked like the wild man from Borneo.

He'd told me to stay in a chair quiet all that day, and Mu Lan sat beside me talking. Funny thing, soon as I'd gotten well from the kuntaow a few weeks back, she'd got all sad and mournful like before; but now I was sick and she was taking care of me, she was all gay and happy again. And she told me stories of how when she was a little girl back in the country when a tiger was around, you mustn't mention his name or he'd come and kill you; you must call him Mr. Stripes. And she told me how the natives said monkeys knew how to talk just as good as people, but they wouldn't because if people found out they could talk they'd put the monkeys to work.

And then Rani and her mother come in for a little while, and Mu Lan looked awful sad like she did before, and left.

Rani and me talked about the reincarnation again, how maybe we'd been a couple of eagles. It was like a game for me, but course for her it was true. And she said she was sure she'd been a fish some time, because she loved the water so. And I said how I'd always liked swimming, going in every chance I had at the swimming hole back home, and how maybe I'd been a fish, too, swimming around, looking after her, and keeping away the sharks. And I said how even if I was a fish no bigger than a finger I'd go into a shark's mouth to save her. And she smiled and took my hand when her mother wasn't looking.

And then Rani left and the kuntaow doctor come and took out the needles, and the pain in my head was finished.

Well, a couple of nights later it's pretty stormy, and I ain't sleeping so good. And all of a sudden I jump out of bed with the feeling that something's terrible wrong. And I look out the window, and I see the lights on shore going past. We're moving.

And I yell to G.B. to wake up, and race outside. The sky's all black and there's a gale blowing, and I can see the wharf where we'd been tied moving farther and farther away. And then I can see we're heading right onto some rocks across the harbor that'll smash the boat to pieces.

I grab a rope as G.B. comes running up, and I try to figure out what to do. We're way past the line of wharves now, sweeping straight to the rocks, and it looks like we're goners. And then I see a oil dock that comes a lot farther out than the others, and I can see we're going to pass close.

I'm a pretty good riverman, I guess. I used to help grandpa when I was a kid in the hills making the log rafts he'd float down to the sawmills. And I made a loop in the line, and waited till we came to just the right place by the oil dock and tossed. It caught on a iron cleat, and pulled awful hard for a minute, and I thought it was going to break. But it held, and soon as we could, we got out another line.

The storm got worse, but it was over by daylight, and we got a Chinese running a tugboat to tow us back to our wharf. And then we had a chance to see what had made the mooring lines let go; they'd been cut through smooth as velvet with an axe.

That afternoon we went to town and when we come back I was holding one end of a chain. And the other end, like Alf had told me, was fastened to the collar of a Great Dane.

Chapter VIII

The dog was a big fellow, looked so gentle everybody wanted right away to pat him on the head. But he was really a devil; if you gave him half a chance, he'd tear you to pieces. And we didn't have him a week when Rani goes to feed him a piece of meat, and he turns on her like a leopard and takes a bite out of her leg. Course I felt awful, and I rushed her off to the Dutch doctor, and he bound up her leg and gave her what they call a inoculation. But I was just sick about it, because it was a real bad bite.

I asked Rani what I could do to make up for it, what present I could give her, because I sure had to do something after a terrible thing like that.

And her mother says quick, like she had the answer all ready, "Maybe you could give her a sewing machine, Tuan."

I knew that a American sewing machine was what the women there wanted more than anything; if you had a sewing machine it was like you was getting into society.

So I ask Rani if that's what she'd like, and her big eyes shine like jewels. "O Tuan, a sewing machine would make me more happy than anything in the world," she says.

"And maybe you could give her a bolt of yellow silk to make a dress," says her mother quick.

"I think I would rather have blue silk, Mama," says Rani.

So next day I went out and bought her the machine and the silk. And her eyes shine like the jewels again.

I never seen anybody could use their eyes the way Rani did. She could show loving, hating, being happy, being sad, just with her eyes, without saying a word. And she could change from one to the other like lightning. And when she didn't want you to see what she was thinking she could drop a kind of veil over her eyes, and for a minute her face'd get like a mask. And then the mask'd go away, and it'd be Rani again.

She kept the machine on the boat where everybody could see it, and whenever she could she'd sit there sewing beautiful clothes for herself. And I could see that my giving her the machine hurt Mu Lan bad, and I explained to Mu Lan that it was because of the dog bite, and I'd get her one, too, if she wanted it.

"I have no need of a machine, Tuan," she told me. But when she said it I could see her eyes were full of tears.

Course I took the dog back in a hurry. And that was the end of the Great Danes.

Well, it gets to be time for our first graduation, and except for the trouble about the Harmonious Daggers and the priests, things at the school couldn't have been better. G.B. gets some fancy diplomas printed, and he makes what they call a graduation speech, saying to the students he knows they'll all be big successes now, and a credit to the school. He ends up by pointing to the picture of the Presidents in the Black Hills.

"Remember," he says. "This is your motto. It can be you the same as them. Live so you'll be carved in a mountain."

And he sits down, and everybody applauds; there's so much noise it's like the hoofs in a Western movie when the cattle's stampeding. And then he hands out the diplomas and everything goes off fine.

The graduation must have made the Harmonious Daggers mad, because it wasn't more than twenty-four hours afterward they started acting out in the open. I guess they'd got tired of trying the other way.

I'm walking back with Teddy from town, when all of a sudden half a dozen of the Dagger fellows come riding up on the green bicycles; and they jump off, and in a second one of them's on me and one of them's on Teddy. I start fighting the one that jumped me, and get him down, and Teddy does the same, and then the other four come at us, and looks like we're finished. And then I see Teddy take the towel he's wearing around his neck—all the Menang people wear them that way to soak up the sweat. And he dips the towel in a bucket of water standing there, and begins fighting off all the four. I remembered he'd told me if you knew kuntaow, you could kill a man with a wet towel, even a wild boar, he said.

He was really holding them off, that Teddy; he was taller than most of the others and he sure looked like a straw man, fighting off a bunch of hungry wild cattle trying to eat him like hay. And a big crowd gathers to watch, but they don't do anything. Because it's like when you have family trouble at Muleshoe—they used to call it feuding—nobody ever called the sheriff or nobody interfered. And then one of the fellows ran off to his bicycle and came back with one of

105

those kuntaow cat-of-nine-tails made of the lead bars and chains; and Teddy got it away from him, and began battling with that.

He'd have had them all knocked out, when maybe a dozen more of the Daggers rode up, and joined the others in the fighting. Of course we wouldn't have had a chance after that, if a lot of fellows from another secret society, the Celestial Tigers, hadn't happened to come up the street. They were a smaller society than the Daggers, but they were the next biggest in Menang, and they hated the Daggers like poison. They were always looking for one of the Daggers so they could do him in. It was kind of like the Hatfields and McCoys, I guess, used to be back home. Well, they jumped in and pretty quick the Daggers was racing off, and some of them were beat up pretty bad.

The chief of the Celestial Tigers was a giant of a fellow with little eyes and a thick neck and head; he kind of looked like the Malay rhinoceros they had out in the jungle. He'd been watching Teddy fighting, and now he came over to where we were standing and said something to Teddy in Chinese.

We go on back to the boat and Teddy's yellow face is all lit up with a kind of pink glow, like the sun when it's first rising over the Menang mountains. "O Tuan, I am very happy," he says. "When I think that only a few months ago you pulled the miserable creature that was I out of the clutches of the River God. And now this honor has come to me."

I asked him what'd happened.

"It is the greatest day since I have been born, Tuan. And I owe it all to the school. The chief with whom I was speaking, the great one with a head and chest like a buffalo, has seen me fighting today. He has asked me to become a Celestial Tiger."

A few days later he told me how the night before he'd

gone out with the big fellow and the others to a rice field in the moonlight, and they pricked his arm for blood, and he swore blood brotherhood with everybody there. And then he pulled back his shirt and showed me the new tattoo mark on his chest, a crouching tiger.

After that we wasn't bothered by the Harmonious Daggers for a little while. I guess they wasn't feeling too good after the beating they took from the Tigers. And now they knew Teddy was one of them, and we had some friends, I guess they figured things were different, and they'd go kind of slow.

Well, a few more months passed, and we graduated a second class, and all the time the school was getting more and more popular. And with our parties and the jazz dancing once a week, and the students going out and talking, we were really beginning to change that town. A lot of the tea-houses had the jukeboxes and the pin ball machines now, and more were wanting them. We sold or rented all we had, and sent to the States for more.

And a lot of the temples—there were a couple of hundred—saw how fine Tak Thong was doing at the temple of the Sleeping Buddha. And they said they wanted the loudspeakers out in front, just the same as him. So we kind of went into the loudspeaker business and got plenty of them, from Singapore and Hong Kong and anywhere we could. When it come time for prayers now nobody could say they didn't know; you could hear the temple bells ringing out on the loudspeakers all over town. I sure liked to hear them. It was real pretty.

But looked like the old-timers didn't understand at all and it was making them madder and madder.

Teddy, who was climbing up in the Celestial Tigers fast, and knew everything that was going on now, started talking to me about it one afternoon when we were out in the trishaw, riding past the snake temple.

"We must be watchful, Tuan," he said. "The high priest here and the mullahs have had many meetings with the Tunku's brother. I think they will be striking again very soon, Tuan. And this time it will be a real war."

Rani and me kept getting along fine. I'd sit with her while she sewed her fancy sarongs on the machine, with her mother looking on all the time, smiling and eating coconut. And she'd wrap one of the sarongs around her and fix a wreath of flowers in her golden hair and say to me, "Am I beautiful in this, Tuan?"

And then before I had a chance to answer she'd try another, and say, "Or am I more beautiful in this one, Tuan?"

Or sometimes she'd fix her hair the way girls do back home, kind of wrapped around on top with little combs the way she seen in the movies, and ask, "Or is this the most beautiful, Tuan?"

I couldn't ever tell which way was best. To me it didn't make any difference. All I knew she was the most beautiful thing in the world, and I was getting crazier about her every minute.

But things with Mu Lan wasn't good at all. Ever since the dog bit Rani and I'd bought the sewing machine I was getting worried about her. Like I said, I'd figured we were just friends, but I guess she was in love with me bad.

We'd sit and practice the Kentucky Mountain songs like we did before, and I taught her some new ones, like *The Roving Gambler*. And she sang pretty as ever, but she didn't seem to enjoy it like old times.

And then one day she takes out a kind of Chinese zither she played, kind of like the zither Ma had when I was a kid in the hills. And she gives the zither to me, and smiles the way she used to and says, "Maybe I can teach you a Chinese song, Tuan."

It's a sad song, all about a beautiful girl in Menang loves a young fellow makes wonderful pottery, the finest in all the islands. And she's going to marry him and help him make the pottery even better, when all of a sudden he gets pneumonia or something and dies. And she loves him so much she just pines and pines away, sitting all day looking at his beautiful pottery and knowing how there won't ever be any more. And then finally she can't stand it any longer, and she goes to the volcano, and throws herself into the crater. And that way she can be with him and help him make pottery in the other world.

I try hard to learn the song to please Mu Lan. I can get the notes all right, but course it don't sound like music. It's more like a cat running around the shelves of a kitchen, knocking down all the tin pans. And when I try to sing the Chinese words it's worse. But she laughs like the ice in the creek again, the first time in a long while, and I could see it made her happy, even if it was only for a minute.

I sure wished I could have done different about her. I thought about her and Rani and me all the time.

And sometimes I'd wake up in the middle of the night and hear a Chinese or Malay girl off in the distance singing and playing what they call a lute, and you could tell the song was about love. And I'd get to thinking about how queer love was, and the funny way God made men and women so they got all tangled up and unhappy. And I'd get to thinking maybe when He was making them, He fell asleep and somebody came along, the Devil maybe, and mixed up the cement he was using. Cause if it wasn't a mistake He sure ain't as smart as people give Him credit for being.

Mu Lan was giving me coffee in the kitchen on the boat one afternoon when a pigtailed little girl that's a cousin of hers comes in for a minute; and when she's gone, Mu Lan turns to me all gay the way she used to be.

"O Tuan, there will be a Chinese wedding at the house of my rich uncle," she says. "His grandson is to marry the daughter of a rice merchant. My uncle has invited you if you wish to come."

I'd been wanting to see one of those weddings bad, because the way I told you, I always like to find out about different things. And besides I could see Mu Lan wanted me to, so course I said I'd go.

Well, the time for the wedding comes about two weeks after, and the night before Mu Lan's all smiling and excited.

"O Tuan, you cannot sleep long tonight," she says. "The astrologers have studied the horoscopes of the bride and the groom, and they have found the hour when the wedding must take place. They will be married at half past three in the morning."

Well, she and her giggling sister called for me in a trishaw at fifteen minutes before three. And I sure thought it was pretty funny, going to a wedding that way in the middle of the night. We rode through the dark streets with not a soul anywhere, and pretty soon we got to the house with the courts like the Chinese boxes. And the bride was there all fixed up like a queen with a young Chinese that was the groom, looking kind of stiff and silly, just like the man does at a wedding back home.

The bridegroom gave the bride a beautiful pair of earrings and put them on her. And then there was some kind of ceremony I didn't understand. And Mu Lan's uncle opened up something in the wall looked like a little ivory graveyard full of little tombstones Mu Lan said was the tablets of her ancestors. And the bride and groom knelt before them, and the groom told the ancestors he was bringing a new member into the family, and she'd look after them fine. And the uncle wrote down her name by the side of the name of the young Chinese and by doing that they were married.

We went around and saw all the presents, and then we sat down and ate. I thought I'd eaten before, but that was like turnip greens and corn pone compared to this. But I didn't enjoy it at all. Because all the old ladies kept looking at the bride, and looking at Mu Lan, and then at me. And they'd smile at her, and say "You next." And I kept thinking about when we came before and what a fine time we'd had then before I'd ever met Rani. And I could see how sad Mu Lan was looking now, and I knew she was thinking the same way.

It got worse and worse with the old ladies' teasing, and after a while I could see it was hard for her to keep from crying. And I told the people at the table I had a kind of upset stomach from the Army, and I got out of there with her and her sister as soon as I could.

We didn't talk hardly at all going back, and her sister didn't giggle once. I sure was sorry I'd come.

A couple of days later what they call the Feast of The Hungry Ghosts came along when everybody sets out things to eat for their relatives that have died; and they put out plenty extra, too, in case a beggar ghost is there maybe would want to steal something. It's a big holiday and the school is closed, and G.B. gets up early to drive off with Alf to the country and go fishing. I walk to the post office to get our mail before it shuts up and spend the day fixing the boat, doing a little painting and carpenter work it's been needing. And that night I go out to the Happy World to see Rani.

I don't stay late, because her brother's come from one of the other islands, and they're having a kind of family reunion, so I walk on back to the school. And I see Mu Lan with Mock Duck, not gone home yet, standing by the water. And Mu Lan's holding a little paper boat, with a little pile of cooked rice in the front, and in the back is a colored candle. And she writes something on a red piece of paper and wraps it around the candle; and then she lights the wick and puts the boat in the water.

"What you doing, Mu Lan?" I say.

"It is the Night Of The Hungry Ghosts, Tuan," she says. And she looks at me awful sad, and blows on the boat to make it move away from the shore. And then she walks down the wharf a little way and stands there, kind of murmuring to herself, and watches the boat drift out to sea.

"What's she doing?" I whisper to Mock Duck.

He answers in his funny high voice, like he's singing a Chinese song. "She is praying to the Hungry Ghosts, Tuan. On this night if you put your troubles on a little boat and the Hungry Ghosts are listening they will come to eat the rice in the boat and your troubles will all float away."

They went home right after, and I walk on up the gangplank. I could hear G.B. was back, and I go to his room. And I'm sure shocked when I see him. All the blood is gone from his face and arms; it's like he's covered himself all over with ashes, the way I seen the Chinese do for their funerals. And he's throwing clothes into a suitcase like a dog digging up a fox.

"What's the matter, G.B.?" I say. "You been seeing one of them Hungry Ghosts?"

"I ain't seen one. I'll be one," he answers. "If I don't get out of this town in ten minutes."

I guess I turn as pale as him. I can't say a word for a minute. "What . . . what you mean?" I ask.

"I mean it's that letter from Singapore you left in my room this morning. There's a boat leaving here for Jakarta right away. If I don't catch it, I'm a dead fish."

I start shaking worse than the time I was working on the section gang and got malaria. "What you done?" I ask. "Is it . . . woman trouble again?"

"It ain't woman trouble and I ain't done anything," he

says. "It's what somebody done to me. I didn't tell you because I thought I'd make a lot of money and surprise you, and then use it to buy a new boat for the school or something."

He takes some socks from a drawer and tosses them into the suitcase. "I been partners on the side with a Rumanian fellow in Singapore that run away from the Communists. He was selling a new kind of trading stamp there, better than any kind of stamps anywhere. They gave you a Rolls Royce automobile pretty near if you bought half a dozen cans of pork and beans. These stamps was better than money in the bank."

He throws in his shirt that's got the little red race horses on it and a fancy tie that's covered with little baseballs and dice. "The Rumanian wrote me the business was doing fine and he was selling plenty. When those smart-aleck, English-trained police they got there started noseying around and pretended to buy some groceries. And then they went to get some of the fancy premiums advertised in the stamp books, and they couldn't even get a box of matches. The Rumanian had kind of borrowed all the money to spend on booze and sing-song girls."

He gave me the letter I'd brought him to read. "The letter's from the fellow runs the bar in Singapore where I met the Rumanian. It says he skipped out two days ago, they don't know where, and the police are coming from Singapore to get me in the morning. I knowed I never should have trusted one of them Communists. That's the trouble with me. I'm always trusting people."

I began helping him pack, and I tell you I could hardly hold a shoelace, I was shaking so all over. I'd had bad news in my life before; but this was so sudden and so terrible I couldn't believe it. I thought my brain'd bust.

Here I was losing a friend that was like a father to me, I guess forever. And besides he was leaving the school in my hands, after he'd been pretty near the whole show. It was like the time in the cotton factory when a flywheel broke, and a big piece of the belt hit me in the back. I was so numb for a couple of days you could have driven those acapuncture needles all the way through me and I wouldn't have felt a thing.

Well, in a few minutes G.B. got packed up, and Amok that was still around ran and got a auto. And we drove to a rusty little freighter that was tied up at a dock. We talked till they blew the whistle about what I'd do with the school, and all the good times we'd had. And I guess if we'd have been girls we'd have both busted out crying.

And the whistle blew again, and a sailor came around beating a gong and trying to say, "All ashore that's going ashore." But he couldn't say it right because Chinese can't say r's. And it sounded so funny we both started laughing.

And then I get to feeling blue again and start down the gangplank. "I'll be thinking of you every minute, G.B.," I say. "I'll do the best I can, but there's only one G.B. in the world."

And I step onto the dock, and the plank goes up and he smiles at me, kind of pitiful, with his eyes like a sheep lost in a blizzard. And then as the boat starts to move he changes quick, as if he don't like being gloomy, and starts laughing again.

"Don't marry more than five women till I get back," he calls. "Only four's legal here. But they give you one extra and a box of groceries if you pay cash."

And all the sailors start laughing their heads off. And the boat moves farther away.

"Don't take in any wooden nickels or rubber checks," he calls. And everybody laughs again.

And then the boat goes out into the darkness and is gone.

I rode back in the car by myself, numb all over again like

when the belt hit me. And I never felt so lonesome in my life.

And then the car got to our boat, and I walked aboard. And I looked around and thought of all the things I'd have to do with the school, now that G.B. wouldn't be there any more, and I felt a thousand times worse.

It was like the space comic when the fellow landed all alone on the moon and then some space enemy did something to the rocket that was to take him back to earth, and he knew now he'd never get home.

I was sitting in my room, getting ready for bed, though I knew I wouldn't sleep a wink, when I heard Teddy pedaling up the wharf in his trishaw. That was kind of funny, because he never came to the boat so late, and I knew right away something was wrong.

A minute later there's a knock on my door.

"Come in," I say, and Teddy hurries inside, and his yellow face has queer white patches all over, like a pancake when the dough ain't baked right.

"O Tuan, there is bad news," he says. "The priests and the mullahs have been talking this night of the Hungry Ghosts with the Tunku's brother and the Harmonious Daggers. One of our Celestial Tigers was listening all through their meeting. They say they can stand what is happening in Menang no longer. In two or three days, when the moon and the stars are right, they are coming to destroy the school."

Chapter IX

For a couple of days after G.B. left I went around kind of crazy, I guess. I felt like one of those big worms you cut up with a shovel sometimes digging, and the different parts go every which way and you can't tell which is the head and which is the tail.

And then a Chinese detective came from Singapore looking for G.B. and I told him how I knew G.B. better than anybody and he was a wonderful fellow, was just unlucky the way he'd get blamed for the things that other people done. I told him how fine G.B. was teaching the school, and how he'd told me he'd cut his throat before he did anything wrong. But the Chinaman didn't pay much attention.

And that night I had to think about something different.

I was sitting in my room, trying to figure out all the things I had to do with the school when I hear Teddy's trishaw coming up the wharf, faster than I ever heard it before. And I hear him running up the gangplank, and then he bursts into the room.

"Get up, Tuan!" he shouts. "They are coming!"

I jump from my chair and look out the window, and I see a red glow in the sky. The glow gets bigger and then I hear a funny kind of noise in the distance. And I grab my gun from off the wall and run out on the deck. And Mu Lan and Mock Duck and Amok who are working late come running out, too. And Mock Duck and Amok grab hold of anything they can and stand waiting back of me. The noise comes closer and pretty soon I can see it's a bunch of fellows playing gongs and beating big brass cymbals. And behind them's a regular parade of maybe two or three hundred people, all carrying torches and singing some kind of queer song that makes your blood turn to ice.

Walking at the end was the head priest of the snake temple in his red silk robe, the fellow with the round face and body looked like one of the smiling little Buddhas with the fat naked stomachs you can buy for a dime. And with him were the other priests and mullahs that had come to the boat before, the Malays and the Chinese with the long white beards and a couple of Hindus.

The round face of the little Buddha wasn't smiling now; he looked like the high priest in the space comic when he's getting ready to sentence the earth man to a human sacrifice. In the middle of the fellows with the torches I could see a bunch of men carrying something on a kind of litter, covered with a black cloth. I could tell it was big and awful heavy; it looked maybe like a coffin.

The parade stops right in front of the boat, and some of the men start picking up pieces of wood and logs laying on the wharf and put them in a pile. And I see the fellow that looks like Fu Manchu standing like a statue, watching.

"What they going to do, Teddy?" I ask.

He shakes his head. "I do not know, Tuan," he says. "Whatever it is, it is not good."

A minute later the fat priest calls out something in Chinese, and the fellows with the litter come forward. And they take off the black cover from what looks like a coffin and then I see what they're carrying. It's one of our jukeboxes, all shiny with metal and polished mahogany they've got hold of some way. And they take it off the litter and set it on the ground; and they begin piling the wood and the logs they've collected close around it, the way when you're roasting something in a fire. And then I knew what was going to happen; it was just like I seen once in a moving picture about Joan of Arc, when they were getting ready to burn her at the stake.

The gongs and the cymbals get louder and louder and the chanting shriller and shriller; and the priest makes some kind of sign with his hand and then he picks up a torch.

"I'm going to stop 'em," I say, and I start down the plank.

But Teddy and Mock Duck and Amok run forward and they hold me back.

"You must not go, Tuan," Teddy says. "They will tear you to pieces."

I see how they're getting wilder and wilder, and how many there are, and I know we haven't got a chance. So I just stand there like I'm turned to stone, the way a hypnotizing fellow selling patent medicine done to a couple of kids once in the drugstore window in Muleshoe. Then the priest lifts the torch, and says some kind of prayer and throws it on the pile, and in a second the wood's all blazing. And then I don't know whether somebody started it or whether it was the heat, but all of a sudden the jukebox sort of groans and it begins to play. It was the kind ran on its own batteries and didn't need no current.

It was a Niagara jukebox—like I said that was the best

119

kind—and when it played it always lit up like a rainbow and looked like water going over the Falls. And this time I'd never seen it shine so bright. You could almost feel the spray splashing.

The mahogany part of the box catches then and little red flames like needles begin popping up all around, I guess where the paint is burning. And the crowd gives a roar like hungry tigers. The piece the box played was *Wait Till the Sun Shines, Nellie*, that's a old-fashioned piece, but all fixed up now for jazz, you know the way they do. It's a awful sad piece, and when you hear the singer kind of sobbing out the words, "Wait till the clouds roll by," and you see that beautiful box with the Falls all lit up, burning to death, it sure makes a lump come into your throat. It's just like it was a human being.

The flames get higher and higher, but still it keeps on playing; like it was trying to be brave and wasn't going to give in. And then a big flame shoots up from the top and it starts a kind of rattling; it sounds just like a old man when he's laying in bed and dying. And then it gives a awful groan, and for a minute is all still. And then there's a kind of explosion, and a lot of sparks fly up like from a bursting volcano; and then all you can see of the box is the frame, like a fiery skeleton. And then all of a sudden it crumples up, and is nothing but a pile of red coals. And the crowd gives another roar, and the priests and the mullahs move toward the boat, and begin walking up the gangplank.

There are a couple of policemen standing there, but they don't do a thing; and I know it's no good asking them to help. Course they're on the side of the crowd.

I tell Mu Lan to move inside, and I go to meet the people coming up the plank, and Teddy and Mock Duck and Amok are right behind me.

The fat little priest is leading the others and he stops at the edge of the boat.

I hold my gun ready, and I'm all tight like a wire, the way I was when a man in the section gang when I was railroading went crazy and come at me with a sledge hammer.

"What you want?" I say, and I hear the words, but they're so cold and far off it don't sound like it's me that's saying them.

I know the priest talks English good, but this time he don't answer me. Instead he says some words to Teddy in Malay, and Teddy stands there like he's a wound up wire, too, and then he what they call translates.

"He says they want no more trouble, Tuan," Teddy tells me, and I can see he's watching the priest and the others every second, ready to spring like a leopard. "He says they have burned the jukebox as a warning. He says you must leave Menang."

I grip my gun tighter. I come from country where there's plenty of shooting, and my blood is boiling after what they done to the jukebox and now what they're saying to me. But I hate shooting, and I ain't ever shot anybody, and I don't want to start now.

I watch the priest standing by the boat chewing betel nut, and I think a minute. And then I answer him the way I figure G.B. would have done if G.B. had been there.

"Tell him to go chew his betel nut somewhere else," I say to Teddy. "I'll leave when I'm good and ready."

Teddy tells him, and when the priest answers his words are like he was cutting granite.

"He says this is your last chance, Tuan," Teddy tells me. "He says if you do not agree to leave tonight like your partner has done, they will burn the boat, like they burned the jukebox. And he does not know when the people are so angry what evil they will do to you. . . . He says they will wait for your answer."

The priest and the others go down the plank again, and

stop out on the wharf. And then some of the men begin to throw rocks and things, but it don't do any damage.

Teddy keeps looking and looking off into the distance, and when I asked him why, he said he was watching for the Celestial Tigers. He'd told them to be expecting trouble, and they were supposed to be coming around.

The crowd on the wharf gets bigger and bigger, but there isn't a sign of a Celestial Tiger anywhere.

Everything's quiet for maybe half an hour while the priests and the others stand waiting. And then the priest calls out a command, and I see a new bunch of fellows carrying something whose glass top shines in the dark. And they bring it over to where they burned the jukebox and get ready to put it on the coals. And this time it's a pin ball machine.

They start pulling the handles and making the bells ring and the lights flash, because it's on batteries, too.

I know now they'd broke into the Cafe of the Sixth Heaven, started by a little Chinaman was in the school for a while, and rented the jukebox and the machine from us.

It's what they call the "Old Glory" machine—I guess you seen them maybe—lights up the red and white stripes of the American flag when you roll a good number, and makes all fifty stars flash like fireworks when you hit a winner.

"That's one machine I ain't going to see 'em burn," I say. "I'm going down and bring it up here on the boat."

And I fire my gun in the air to scare them off, and run down with Teddy behind me. And I guess they're scared of the gun, or maybe they're surprised; and we grab the machine and bring it up the plank, and then the crowd gives a howl like a bunch of tigers again, and they start closing in. And I stand at the plank with my gun pointed at them, and my finger ready on the trigger.

I don't know what would have happened, except just

then there's a terrific flash of lightning and a bolt of thunder that shakes the boat like an earthquake. And then the rain comes down in one of them sudden storms they have all through the islands where it don't seem like rain at all; it's like a dam burst its walls and all the water fell on you. And the lightning flashes in all kinds of colors, green, and red, and purple, and orange, in half a dozen places at once, like the world is coming to an end. And everybody ran off as fast as they could, because they're terrible scared of bad storms; they think it's the gods are mad at them and it's a bad Feng Shui or something. And now it's a special bad sign that the astrologers had made a mistake; the moon and the stars were wrong.

They got a good reason to be scared of the storms; the lightning in Menang kills more people than the snakes and the tigers put together. I was talking to Bertie and Alf about it once, and they said it's because the island is full of radium. And course if you've ever read a space comic you know that radium'll draw the electricity from the sky every time. That's how they shoot the space death rays and things.

The thunder and lightning lasted pretty near four hours, and course by the time it's over everybody in the crowd's gone home. The Celestial Tigers came a little later and told Teddy they were sorry but they got in a fight with another bunch of the Daggers in another part of town, and couldn't get away.

I went to bed, but I didn't sleep so good. Because I knew when the old-timers figured the stars were right they'd be coming again.

And then I started thinking what I was going to do about the teaching, now G.B. was gone. And I remembered about Mr. Bascom, the funny old man from New Orleans.

"I'll find him first thing in the morning," I say to myself. "Looks like he's just the fellow we need."

Next morning at breakfast Mock Duck asks me for some whisky. I'm surprised, because I know he's not a drinker, and I ask him why he wants it.

"It is for the Kitchen God, Tuan," he says. "In my sleep he appeared and told me it was he who brought the storm last night. And he said also he is tired of the rice I give him. He says perhaps it will taste better if with it he has some whisky."

I gave him a little out of the bottle, and right away saw him smearing it on the lips of the god.

I go looking for Mr. Bascom soon as I finish eating. The place he told us was in a part of town along the beach where the Malay people were living. And at first I thought it was the wrong address, because the neighborhood kept getting poorer and poorer; nothing but little wooden houses up on stilts, each with a little wooden porch where women were pounding things to eat, and a lot of kids were playing. And pretty soon the people were all fishermen, with big nets hanging in front of the porches and big piles of fish drying in the sun. And I kept asking and pretty soon I find the house, with seven little girls playing on the porch and two dogs and a fat pig playing around them. And a big fat Malay woman was sitting there, peeling a kind of cucumber.

She gives a big smile when I ask if Mr. Bascom lives there. "The Tuan is inside," she says. And I go on through the door.

The room's full of sacks of rice and dried fish and some funny kind of brown meal. And there's a couple of fishing traps and rakes and hoes standing in the corner. Instead of a place to live it looks more like a warehouse. There's a couple of native beds of straw, and a couple of babies sleeping on one of them. But off in a corner is a neat bed made of wood with a white pillow and nice white sheets. And by it Mr. Bascom is sitting in a broken chair, reading some kind of book. He's all dressed up in black pants, with a crease you could use to slice bread; and he's wearing a kind of stiff white shirt and a bow tie like the rich people have when they're going to a big party. And instead of shoes he's wearing Chinese wooden slippers and he ain't got a coat on.

As I walk in all the seven little girls that were outside follow me and stand there watching and giggling. And the two dogs come in and look and then the fat pig, too.

The old fellow's reading so hard he don't hear me; and then I call his name, and he looks up and sees me surprised. And his face lights like an electric bulb just when it's blowing out.

"Mister Oral!" he says, and then he looks embarrassed. "I am sorry. I am not properly dressed. I was not expecting visitors."

And he goes to the side of the bed where I see a few clothes hanging, and he puts on the coat with the handkerchief in the pocket and a pair of pointed black shoes.

"It is the only coat I have left so I must preserve it as much as I can," he says. "My income lately has been so straitened. And the same applies to my shoes. The situation is somewhat better as applied to trousers. Whenever I required a suit I always purchased two pair."

He gives me his chair—it's the only one in the room. And the seven girls sit down giggling on the floor around me. And the dogs and the pig sit down, too. And then Mr. Bascom hesitates, and takes a place on the bed.

"I am sorry," he says, looking at the girls and the babies asleep on the bed next to him. "It is somewhat crowded here. But the cost of the inns in the town is prohibitive. And Mrs. Kanaka is very kind. . . . Perhaps you will have some tea."

He called to the fat lady outside and she came in, all smiles, and put a teapot on the little Malay stove in the corner.

While we were waiting for it to heat a big shiny beetle

125

came out of a hole in the wall and walked across the floor. The old man jumped and grabbed a can of insecticide and gave it a single squirt. And the beetle ran off toward the wall it'd come out of and disappeared down the hole.

Mr. Bascom shook his head. "Ah, these beetles," he said. "They drive me to despair. Since I have been in this house they have eaten one coat and three pairs of trousers. I think I would prefer man-eating tigers."

A minute later some big ants came out from under a board and crawled across the room like the beetle. Mr. Bascom started to pick up the can, and then put it down. "These insecticides grow so expensive. With the inflation in America I must learn to tolerate the ants, and concentrate on the beetles and the spiders."

The fat woman set the tea down before us.

Mr. Bascom drank his slow. "We had wonderful teas at Miss Fairlee's school," he said. "At five o'clock every Thursday. All the elite of New Orleans came. As I told you, my sister in 1913 was the queen of the Mardi Gras ball."

I told him I wanted him to come to the school, and he looked very happy. We got ready to start out so he could look it over when he happened to glance down at his pants.

"The crease is not good enough," he says. And he goes to a chair where a newspaper's under a heavy sack of rice, and pulls out a pair of trousers. "Mrs. Kanaka always presses them this way," he says. "Sometimes she uses a sack of dried fish. Alas, I cannot teach Mrs. Kanaka the use of an iron."

And he pulls a string he's got rigged up by the bed, and draws a burlap curtain. And when he comes out he's got on the other trousers and a flower in his coat, and he's carrying the black hat besides. And we walk on toward the boat and we talk about what he'll teach.

"I think perhaps if you wish I will be best teaching the subjects I taught at Miss Fairlee's," he says. "Especially the young ladies. Your school is a school for success and this is most appropriate. To the Malay and Chinese girl marriage is important above all else. And the graduates of Miss Fairlee's where I played a not inconsiderable part were noted for their successful marriages."

He tipped his hat and bowed as some fancy dressed Chinese passed in a expensive automobile. And they bowed back, though I could tell they sure didn't know him.

"I make it a practice to bow to the gentry here," he says. "I think it helpful to international relations."

He straightened the flower in his lapel, and began to talk about the school again. "There is nothing so lovely as a beautiful girl whose charm has been enhanced by proper training. As I told you, I taught deportment and manners and elocution and singing and dancing. It was said I was excellent at teaching the waltz and quite expert in a gay Polish dance known as the Varsuviana. Since being here I have made some inquiry into the local customs. I feel competent to teach the arrangement of flowers and the language of the hands and the etiquette of the fan."

He started next night, and I tell you I sure felt better having somebody there who'd been a big teacher like him. Course the girls were crazy about him. He taught them how American girls walk and talk, even if it was fifty years ago, and gave them the lessons in singing and dancing.

And the men liked him, too, when he taught them elocution. He'd do what they call dramatizing things, the way he said he'd done at the school in New Orleans. When the speakers recited *The Charge of the Light Brigade,* he'd have somebody shooting off pistols; when they did Marc Antony's speech over Caesar's dead body, he made them have a coffin, just like it was a theater.

He was sure good, that Mr. Bascom. When he showed them how to do the burying speech, you'd think you were sitting on the benches there in Rome, right in the middle of all those Roman people. I knowed a fellow come from Rome once in the Army. He could sure eat spaghetti.

Mr. Bascom had been there maybe a week and I was getting worried about the Harmonious Daggers and the oldtimers coming back, when something big happened again. Like I said, Teddy'd been going along so fast in the Celestial Tigers you couldn't keep up with him no way. And then all of a sudden the chief of the Tigers died, and of course he being Chinese they had a terrific funeral.

Teddy invited me to the Tigers' society house to watch the funeral start; and you never saw a funeral like that one. It was like a big circus parade with maybe a couple of thousand people. First there came a Chinese band playing the cymbals and gongs; and then the family wearing what they call sackcloth, looked like they took off all their clothes and put on cement sacks instead. And one of them was carrying a picture of the dead man on a pole and another was carrying a lighted lantern; that was to show him the way when it was dark in the other world, they said.

After that came a big truck carrying the coffin, and then a couple of trucks full of food to put on top of the grave so the dead fellow's ghost wouldn't go hungry. And then there were a lot of paper models to be burned after he was buried. There was a fine big paper three-story house for his ghost to live in, with big paper gardens and trees so he could stay in the shade, and paper actors and musicians to keep him happy. There was a big paper Rolls Royce automobile with two paper chauffeurs sitting in the front, each having a month's pay in Bank of Hell money. There was a paper model of the big ocean liner, the *Queen Mary*, in case he wanted to travel on the water. There was millions of dollars in Bank of Hell money, with what they call an accountant to count it on the other side, so none of the devils there could cheat him. And there was a lot of paper Celestial Tigers in case the Harmonious Daggers or somebody else over there got rough and started a fight. There were a couple of flower pieces, too, and wreaths from some of the European people. And one of the wreaths said "Success," because that was the only word on a flower piece the little Chinaman that made it knew.

After that came all the Tigers that belonged to the Society, with Teddy walking with the big fellows right up in the front; and behind them came the dead man's friends, and then a couple of hundred of the paid mourners crying their heads off. And one of them was the mourner that come to the school, and he seen me, and he stopped crying to wave.

It was so interesting that I walked along the road beside the marchers a little way, just to see what happened.

Well, they had gone maybe a block or so, when down the street comes the funeral of a big man in the Harmonious Daggers; and the two funerals meet head on and neither of them'll give way. And before you know it there's the wildest fight you ever saw, like the time in Memphis they were having a big cat show and some joking fellow picked up a truckload of stray dogs and turned them loose where the cats was. This time Teddy was even braver than when he was fighting before. And he got hold of one of the whips made of the lead and chains again, and I'll bet he knocked out twenty people.

I guess this fight was a draw. And both sides kind of licked themselves like the cats after they'd mixed up with the dogs; and then they both went on to the different graveyards where they'd started. But Teddy was the big hero.

I didn't see Teddy till almost twelve o'clock the next day, and I was getting awful worried; I thought maybe he'd been hurt bad. And then he comes hurrying up the gangplank more excited than I ever seen him before.

"Is it the Daggers coming again?" I ask him.

But he smiles and shakes his scarecrow head. "The Celestial Tigers met last night after the funeral, Tuan," he says.

"They had to choose a chief to take the place of him who went to his ancestors. They chose me, Tuan."

And then he got kind of weepy and came up and kissed my hands. "I owe it all to the school and to you, Tuan, my guru. Without you and the school I would be Teddy the miserable trishaw man, lying at the bottom of the river."

Things were quiet with the school for a little while after that. I heard that now Teddy was the head of the Celestial Tigers he'd sent word to the old-timers and the Harmonious Daggers that if they bothered us again he'd wipe them out. And looks like they must have wanted to take it easy for a while because they didn't even come around with the bicycles on the wharf. And I heard that the Tunku's brother was busy now with a pretty Chinese girl swung from a trapeze in a little circus at the Happy World, and had forgot all about Rani.

Things with Rani and Mu Lan was just about the same. Rani was still crazy about the sewing machine. She'd sit by it with her mother whenever she could, and I'd sit close by her talking.

She worked the machine without any shoes on, like all the women there; and one day I was watching her beautiful feet go up and down with the pedals, when her mother suddenly turns to me.

"Maybe you could get her a pair of shoes, Tuan," she says. "A pair of red shoes like the girls wear in the films I have seen. A pair of red shoes would be very nice for her to have when she dances at the Happy World."

"I think I would rather have a pair of gold shoes, Mama," says Rani.

So I got them for her, the prettiest pair in all Menang, looked like solid gold, fit for a queen.

They cost plenty, but when I gave them to her, and saw the wonderful look in her eyes, it was sure worth every penny. She wore them all the time to the classes after that, and everybody said they were beautiful.

About a week after I gave her the shoes, Mu Lan spoke to me when she was serving my breakfast. And her voice was awful quiet.

"My grandmother in the country has been very ill, Tuan. I received a letter from her yesterday asking me to come and stay with her for a month. I will be going tomorrow, Tuan."

She left next day and I was terrible sorry to see her go, even for a little while. Because I was terrible fond of Mu Lan, and I knew I'd sure miss her. And I felt special bad, because even though I knew her grandmother was sick, I knew she wouldn't have gone if it hadn't been for me and Rani. And then I got to thinking maybe it was a good thing; if she was away a month, she'd kind of forget me, and she'd be all right when she got back.

So it looked like except for G.B. having left maybe everything was going to be all right.

Chapter X

Mu Lan got back in a month like she said, and I thought she was going to be the way she was when I first met her. But in a few days she was all quiet and sad again, just like she was when she'd left.

The school, though, kept getting better and better. G.B. had started it off so good, I guess it would have run by itself. I tried to keep it just the way it was when G.B. was around. Whenever something to decide came up, I'd try to think what G.B. would have done and as soon as I could I did it. And nine times out of ten it was perfect.

Mr. Bascom taught the students the inspiration and speaking and getting confidence and all the things like that. Lucky for us I remembered those what they call recordings G.B. made of his voice teaching How to Become a Millionaire, and we'd play them in the class. And if you were outside the door where you couldn't see, you'd think G.B. was still there. And then Mr. Bascom studied the recordings and the book G.B. wrote, and I was sure surprised; after a little while he was pretty near as good as G.B. Though when he jumped up on the desk and shouted, "Leap like a tiger," the way I told him G.B. done, he strained a ligament.

I kept on running the setting-up exercises, and taught the history course again, and like before I sure enjoyed it. Funny thing, this time it started out real good, with maybe twenty people. And I told them like before about the Pilgrims and Captain John Smith and Pocahontas. And then in a couple of weeks, I couldn't figure out why, there was only two or three left. But of course that was besides Mu Lan. She still come every time, even though she'd had the class once.

Mr. Bascom was especially fine teaching the music and the singing. He had them singing all kinds of fancy things, not *My Bonnie Over the Ocean* and *Good Old Summertime* but them big opera songs, like *Carmen* and *Il Trovatore*. And generally always for the Thursday night parties he'd get them to put on clothes like Gypsies and Italians and Greeks. And they'd sing a song from the opera, the way they'd done at the girls' school in New Orleans. And with their Chinese and Malay faces and voices it was sure funny to hear.

The Thursday nights was wonderful after Mr. Bascom took them over. He had the students dressed up so fancy you'd have thought it was one of those affairs like you see in the movies sometimes, when John D. Rockefeller's having a party for Andrew Carnegie and giving away fancy souvenirs and dimes. And when you looked at them waltzing around you'd have thought they were all lords and queens.

"The waltz is the true test of nobility," said Mr. Bascom.

"Show me a peasant girl who can waltz divinely and I will show you someone worthy of being a bride to a king."

He was fine, too, when we had a hillbilly dance, with "Swing Your Partners," and "Do Si Do," and old-fashioned things that way. I ain't too bad as a dance caller and he was better than me. The hillbilly dances made a big hit, too, so we had them a couple of times. It was nice to see the ladies doing "Birdie Fly In, Birdie Fly Out" in their sarongs and their saris.

"Music has its charms the world over," Mr. Bascom said, watching the people whirl around. "Even for the animals. The natives say in Menang that a flute properly played will arrest a charging tiger. For of all the animals, the natives declare, the tiger is the most musical. They say it is because of the tiger's whiskers; when the proper note is struck the whiskers vibrate in sympathy, like the strings of a guitar."

Sometimes at the parties I'd get pretty worried, because the people were so excitable, especially when we'd have the opera singing. The girl acting a gypsy or something'd be getting ready to stick a kitchen knife in the man that'd done her wrong, and she'd get so worked up I was afraid she was really going to kill him. Because Alf and Bertie both said you can never tell what a Malay or a Chinese is going to do when they're holding a knife. A knife kind of drives them crazy, man or woman, they said, like catnip does a cat.

He was sure a funny one, that little Mr. Bascom. I thought I knowed some funny people back in the hills, but they wasn't nothing to him. Fellows in the Army told me there's plenty like him in Charleston, South Carolina, where he said his family came from way back. They say the people live out of this world, but I never been to Charleston to see them. He started a orchestra for the dancing, and he taught them how to play fine. And he'd be in the middle of leading the players or the people singing the opera when he'd see a cockroach or something crossing the floor. And he'd stop the directing, and pick up a can of insecticide and give it a squirt, and go on with the music again.

Insecticide is one of the words in the dictionary I used to like to roll around my tongue, like *blunderbuss* and *mulligatawny*. In the dictionary it come in the middle of the I's. The last word in the I's was *ivy*.

There was a little slump in the school—Mr. Bascom said schools was always going up and down—and I began to get a little nervous. And then I could see Teddy was getting nervous, too. And one day he come with a half a dozen little Chinamen, pretty near as mean looking as Fu Manchu, and said he wanted to put them in the classes. He paid for them like anybody else, and since we'd been losing some people I was sure glad they came. But they weren't very good students and I could see the others were afraid of them and awful jumpy when they were around. The other students'd be all jolly and having a good time, when all of a sudden these new little fellows'd come in, and everybody'd get awful quiet; they'd be like mice when they hear a weasel up above trying to get down in their hole.

I asked Teddy who they were.

"O Tuan, they are some of my men," he says. "They are other Celestial Tigers. I have brought them to study so they can be good Tigers, and fight the Harmonious Daggers better."

Course I'd have liked them to stay but I could see everybody was getting more and more scared. And it got so bad nobody was doing any work. So I had to ask Teddy to tell them how it was and ask them not to come any more.

He looked kind of puzzled, but course he did what I said.

And then the slump got worse, and I got really worried. And Teddy seen how I was, and he come in one afternoon again with maybe a dozen other men, and they all said they wanted to join the school.

These people weren't Celestial Tigers, you could be sure of that. They were big fellows in Menang; Malays, and Chinese, and Hindus—big businessmen, they said. And they were all kind of fat; with Teddy among them, so lean and skinny, it was like he was the human skeleton with a bunch of fat men in a circus side show. They were different than anybody we'd had before, and I was sure glad to see them. But they were the scaredest people you ever saw; if Teddy said a word to them they'd start shaking all over like the women that dance with their stomachs you see in a burlesque show. And funny thing, whenever they came, some Celestial Tigers always were along. The Tigers'd walk with them as far as the gangplank, and then they'd wait outside. And they'd stand there till the big business fellows were through, and then they'd take them home. And sometimes one of the fellows studying would be chanting "Every Man a King" the way the students did every day, and he'd happen to look out the window. And he'd see one of the Tigers waiting there, and kind of choke, and couldn't go on for five minutes. And I'd ask him what was the matter, but he wouldn't say, only start choking worse.

We'd been having daylight classes a while for the people who didn't want to come at night. And one morning one of the businessmen was there, a Chinese with a big balloon of a stomach that ran the main teahouse in town. He was giving Marc Antony's speech about burying Julius Caesar, and was by the coffin, looking down, when Teddy came in carrying a big knife he'd took from the kitchen to cut a piece of wood or something. And the fat Chinaman happened to look up and seen the knife, and he stopped right in the middle of his speech. And he turned kind of purple, and then kind of a funny yellow-green, like a orange that ain't quite ripe. And I thought he was going to have a heart attack.

I put him in a chair, and I give him a drink, and ask him what's the matter. And he breathes hard for a couple of minutes like a dog chasing cows, and looks around to see if Teddy's gone.

"Oh, Tuan, it is terrible," he says. "This new chief of the Celestial Tigers has come to me and the others. And he has said we must pay you the money to enter your school, and become your students as well. I told him I had already paid much protection money to the Harmonious Daggers. In the past if you paid to one society, that was enough; no other payments would be necessary. But this new chief says this is old-fashioned and all is different now."

He looks around for Teddy again and his voice shakes like palm leaves in the wind. "He says also that if I and the others do not come to the school it will be as with these societies always. They will kidnap me and they will cut off an ear and send it to my family as a warning. If I do not heed they will wait a week and send the other ear also; then each day for ten days they will send a finger or a toe, and finally they will send my body."

Course I made Teddy let the fat man and the other fellows go. I was kind of happy, though. About six of the twelve of them liked the school so much they stayed on anyway.

Pretty soon after that the slump ended, I don't know why, and everything was fine again.

Teddy was getting on wonderful as head of the Celestial Tigers. And I guess he got to remembering how G.B. was always talking about doing things in a big way; and how in the States now the big companies was taking over the little fellows one by one, the way a big catfish goes through a school of minnows. He hadn't been running the Tigers a month before they took over the Heaven on Earth Society, and pretty soon they had the Exalted Dragons Society and the Graceful Accomplishments Society, too. And the Tigers were getting bigger and stronger every day, just like what the sign said on the wall.

Gunga Das was getting bigger all the time, too, and him and Teddy had got to be buddies. He'd went into politics, anyway, spite of our trying to stop him. And he was making speeches on street corners, organizing a party that would stand up against the Tunku sometimes and have it like the Democrats and Republicans back home. And the Harmonious Daggers or the police didn't bother them because Teddy fixed it so there was always some Celestial Tigers standing around.

The graduates were opening up all kinds of American things in town now, soda fountains, and milk and hamburger bars. And they started a nice cafeteria where they'd give you a plate of hot cakes and syrup or a pretty good dish of ham and eggs. And one day a week, though it didn't go so good, they had a dish the owner seen in a magazine and thought it had a pretty sound, a New England Boiled Dinner. And the places all had American names, the same way, like Joe Wong's Kansas City Steak House and Ramayana's OK Snack Bar and Billy Wu's Giant Hot Dogs and Mohammed Ali's Chuck Wagon and Charley Toy's Pizza Pie. It kind of made you feel at home. And pretty near every place that opened put in a jukebox and a pin ball machine and sometimes a loudspeaker. And plenty of other places did it, too, so I had to send again to the States for more.

"Your school's doing too bloody good, Oral," says Alf to me at the bar one afternoon when he's washing up some glasses. "They're moving too fast, like I told you. These people have been living their own easy way for 2000 years, and they ain't built for this bloody new way of doing. It's like a piece I was reading in the English paper. If you put ants on Mars and sprayed radium on 'em they'd get big as shepherd dogs and mice'd grow big as elephants. You keep on this way and ain't any telling what'll happen. Only I know it'll be something bloody awful. . . . Russki, if you've got to eat glass, eat the cracked ones, will you? Glasses here are bloody hard to get."

A terrible drought came along now. When it rained in Menang, the way I said, it was like the world was turned upside down; and the sea was up in the sky and God was letting the water spill out. But now it never rained at all. Everybody said it was the atomic bomb they'd exploded out in the islands, and it sure looked like they were right. Everything began drying up and it got so hot your skin felt like the room in a lumber mill where they're drying out the timber.

We'd close up the boat and all go to the beach to cool off whenever we could, Rani and her mother, and Mu Lan and her sister, and Mr. Bascom, too. Even though Mu Lan knew how I felt about Rani, she and Rani had always been pretty good friends. I'd tell Mock Duck and Amok they could come, too, but they weren't interested.

Mu Lan and her sister and Rani's mother didn't have bathing suits so they didn't go in the water. I guess they were too modest besides. But Rani'd go in wearing her sarong, and she was a wonderful swimmer. I guess it was the Malay blood in her, like the Hawaiians or the girls in the South Seas. When she came out of the water with her dripping gold hair and her shining golden body she was so beautiful it kind of made your heart stop beating.

Mr. Bascom wouldn't go in either. He'd just sit there under a big paper umbrella wearing his coat and his stiff shirt and collar, and his clothes would be melting.

"I cannot agree with the popularity of careless dress today," he would say. "Even though at times it may seem to have advantages. I believe it was Lord Chesterfield who once said, 'Careless dress is the certain sign of a loose and careless mentality.'"

We were all out on the beach one afternoon and had brought a lunch and were getting ready to eat. It was a kind of little picnic. I'd just come out of the water and was watching Rani swimming; she'd wanted to stay in a little longer.

The others were watching her, too; it was something you didn't want to miss.

"She is like a beautiful golden fish," said Mr. Bascom. "The golden fish in the fairy story who was really an enchanted princess. It reminds me of a time just before I left home on the beach at Lake Pontchartrain. That is the large lake as you are probably aware that lies near New Orleans. I was staying at my sister's cottage there and a young woman who had been crowned Miss America was giving a swimming exhibition. The cottage belonged to my sister Eleanora Bascom, not my sister Mary Longstreet Bascom. It was Mary Longstreet, not Eleanora, who was the queen of the Mardi Gras ball at New Orleans in 1913."

He picked up the can of insecticide near him and sprayed it at some bull ants crawling toward our lunch. "The ant, I think, is like the scourges of Job, sent by the Lord to keep man humble. I am grateful to the school for the increase in my income. Now I no longer need spare the ants, but can treat them as I treat the beetles and the spiders."

I could tell Rani was getting ready to come in when all of a sudden I saw something queer rippling the water in toward the shore, like the rippling made by a bunch of little fish when they're swimming away from a shark. I couldn't figure out what it was, because I'd never seen it before, and then the rippling came closer.

And Mu Lan who'd been sitting under another paper umbrella, kind of dreaming, wakes up and jumps to her feet. "It is the sea snakes, Tuan!" she calls out, and runs down to the edge of the water.

And then I look again, and see them, and it was a terrible sight. Thousands and thousands of the snakes, colored kind of like coral snakes, and their bite is worse than a cobra.

What makes them come in like that nobody knows; maybe it's something in the water. They are heading right toward Rani, and I race down the beach and call out to warn her; and she hears me and sees the snakes and starts swimming to the shore fast. She was doing all right, and I couldn't see any snakes near her, when all of a sudden she gives a little cry like she's hurt, and right away she stops swimming.

"She's been bit," I say, and a minute later I'm out in the water.

I knew about snake bites from being bit once by a rattler at Muleshoe, and what the doctor told me. Even if Rani could swim after the bite, if she moved around it'd send the poison all through her and she'd be a goner. And then I see there's a big log drifting near her.

"Stay still as you can!" I shout. "Grab on to the log! I'm coming to get you!"

And I begin swimming hard towards her. The snakes were coming in awful fast now, so thick they looked like a ugly red and black carpet. And I began ploughing my way through them and I sure don't like it. I been scared plenty of times, but this was the worst, I guess, since I'd been born. Funny thing, every time I saw one of their ugly heads come out of the water, I kept thinking they looked like Fu Manchu.

Somehow they let me past without biting. I guess they figured I was a big fish or something. And then I saw Rani, holding on to the log like I'd said, but her eyes was just about closed; in another minute she'd have let go and dropped off into the water. I put her on my back, and started through the Fu Manchus, and got her to the bank. And I laid her down easy on the sand as her mother and Mu Lan came running. And Rani's eyes were all closed now, and her body was like ice, and looked like she wasn't breathing.

Like I said, I know about snake bites. I could see where the snake had bit her in the arm a little below her elbow.

And I found a piece of fishing line laying on the ground, and tied it around her arm; and I took my knife and cut the fang marks, and began sucking the blood. But didn't seem like it made any difference, and it looked like she was dead. And her mother and Mu Lan and her sister begin crying. And Mr. Bascom has big tears in his eyes.

And then Mu Lan stops crying and looks off toward some fisherman's houses on stilts a little way up the beach. "O Tuan, there is a Bomo, a witch doctor, who lives there with the fishermen," she says. "I have heard he is wonderful with the bite of the sea snake. Maybe if you take her there he can save her life."

I don't waste any time talking, so I pick Rani up again, and carry her to the stilt houses. And some fishermen come out to help, and they carry her into the Bomo's place, and lay her on a straw mat. And the Bomo comes, a fine old Malay fellow wearing just a sarong and a turban. And he makes a kind of a white paste in a coconut shell and puts it on the bite. And then maybe a dozen Malay women come in and kneel beside Rani and begin singing and praying. And they moan and clap their hands, like the Holy Rollers in the church back at Muleshoe, only they don't do any jumping. And Rani's mother and Mu Lan and her sister pray along with them. And then the Bomo moves off to a corner where there's a big stuffed water snake with kind of green stones in his eyes; and the Bomo puts some rice down by it, and kneels in front of it like it was a god, and begins praying, too. And then he starts wriggling across the floor, and putting out his tongue and hissing, just like a snake would do. And every few minutes he stops and takes more of the paste and puts it on the bite.

I guess they were praying and carrying on that way for maybe over an hour; and then I see Rani's eyes give a little flicker, and pretty soon they're open wide. And in a minute she's sitting up, wondering where she is. And the Bomo looks happy, and all the others are happy, too. Them Malays are sure nice.

We get a trishaw—Teddy wasn't running his any more because he was too big for that—and we get her home where she lives in a little house not far from Mr. Bascom.

And she looks at me awful tired and sweet, and presses my hands tight. "I will never forget, Tuan," she says. "Not to the end of my days."

A couple of days after she was all right I saw her working hard at the sewing machine. She worked at it three or four days, and I thought she was making herself a new dress. And then she finished what she was sewing, and held it up, and a lovely smile come over her face.

"It is for you, Tuan," she said. "Like the shirt of Tuan Gee Bee."

And I seen it was a shirt made all out of silk, and all covered with little gold leopards and tigers, kind of the same way the shirt G.B. had with the little red racehorses. It was beautiful, with as many colors in it I bet as the shirt Joseph had in the Bible when his brothers put him down in the well.

"Maybe you could give her a nice pair of gold earrings now," Rani's mother tells me. "So when you go walking with her they will match the gold in the shirt."

"O Mama, not now," says Rani.

I sure was proud of that shirt. And I wore it all the time when I wasn't doing rough work, morning, noon, and night.

And course after Rani gave it to me I was crazier about her than ever.

It was right after that I noticed a big change in Mu Lan. She'd changed, like I said, after I gave Rani the sewing machine, but that wasn't anything to the way she changed now. She never looked like a pretty Chinese doll you'd just wound any more, hopping around full of life; now it was like the doll was old and the spring was all worn out. When you asked her a question she'd answer you, but the rest of the time she wouldn't say a word. And she was getting paler and paler.

I got awful worried about her, and I felt I sure owed her plenty; it was Mu Lan, by thinking of the Bomo, that really saved Rani from dying.

I noticed one day when she was giving me lunch that she looked paler than ever.

"What's the matter, Mu Lan?" I say. "You look like you're sick or something. Maybe you ought to go and see the Dutch doctor."

She smiles at me kind of sad, the way she always does now. "I am not sick," she says. "The Dutch doctor will not help me, Tuan."

That night her sister came to call for her after school, and they go off somewheres. And I can tell by the way they're acting it's somewhere mysterious they don't want me to know. It happens every night for a week after that, and every morning Mu Lan looks worse. I figure it ain't any use asking where they go, so the next night I decide to try to find out.

They tell me good night and go down the gangplank and start walking along the street by the wharf. And soon as I can without being seen I follow them in the shadows. They go off to a terrible poor part of Chinatown, full of pushcarts selling hot soup and bean curds; it was so crowded with people you wished you had soft paws like a cat instead of shoes, you were so afraid of stepping on somebody's toes.

They come to a kind of little temple, isn't much more than a kind of lean-to; just a wood roof over a patch of cement. It's even fuller of people than the street, packed so tight even a sardine would have hollered. You couldn't figure how anybody there could even draw a breath, unless they all breathed together. At one end, high up, there's a statue of the Monkey God—he was one of the biggest gods at Menang—with a face half man, half monkey, and smiling what they call a Mona Lisa smile. And then at the other end, on a platform way above the crowd was a kind of golden throne; on the throne a young fellow with a thin, bony face was sitting, wearing a beautiful blue robe covered with funny Chinese signs. His thin legs and arms and skinny body was shaking and rolling so hard from side to side you'd think he'd knock all the meat from his bones.

The place is so thick with incense rising from joss sticks everywhere it's hard to see for the smoke; in front of the god there's a giant joss stick maybe six feet long and three inches wide, sputtering and smoking like a volcano, they say will burn for half a year. All around the edges of the lean-to are Chinese men and women beating on gongs and drums. Their faces and their hands and arms are all stony, like the statue of the Monkey God; they look like they've all took opium and are beating the drums in their sleep.

Mu Lan and her sister crowd their way in, and pretty soon the drums and gongs begin to beat like crazy; and the fellow on the throne shakes faster and faster. And pretty soon he's shaking so fast your eyes get all flashy and blurry; like when the film breaks at a show, and the pictures start going wild.

And then things seem to go wrong, and the people begin groaning. And the fellow on the throne rolls like a ship in a storm, and he begins to foam at the mouth. And then all of a sudden he gives a terrible cry, like when somebody's killing a pig; and his body starts jerking all over like he's having a terrible fit.

And then a priest that's there makes a sign to one of them giant Chinese Manchus standing by the wall. And the Manchu picks up a whip maybe ten feet long and swings it around in front of the throne like the drivers of the old mule teams; and that way he whips off the devils that's bothering the gods, but he almost hits half a dozen people.

And then the men and women beat the gongs and the drums till your ears are pretty near cracking.

And then the blue-robed fellow's face starts to change; his eyes and his mouth kind of shrink, and his cheeks begin to squinch up tight. The skin shrivels and shrivels more and more till it looks just like the face of a monkey. And little by little his hands change, too, and they look like they aren't hands any more; his hands now are monkey paws and his fingers are monkey claws.

And then his mouth begins to move, and he starts a queer noise back in his throat that sets you to shivering all over. And the noise gets louder and then you know what it is; it's just like a monkey chattering.

It was pretty terrible, I tell you, seeing a man become a monkey like that. Then a priest comes up and the monkey man begins chattering at him like crazy. The priest listens till he's through and then gives him a long sheet of red paper. And the men and women in the crowd move up one by one and each of them asks a question. The monkey man chatters at them a minute and takes a piece of black chalk and writes something on the red paper with his claw. And the priest gives it to the people waiting, and tells them what it means. And then I see Mu Lan and her sister go up and Mu Lan asks something in Chinese; and the monkey man chatters at her and the claw writes something and the priest gives her the red paper like he did before. And then Mu Lan and her sister move back into the crowd.

They leave soon after that, and I decide I better go right along with them; it's a pretty rough neighborhood, and there are a lot of tough-looking fellows around. So I walk fast and in a minute catch up.

Mu Lan when she sees me jumps like a quail that's been shot.

"Tuan!" she bursts out, and that's all she can say.

I'm kind of mad now, I guess because I'm worried. "You

got no business in this part of town, Mu Lan," I say. "You and your sister might get hurt. What you doing, seeing that crazy monkey fellow anyway?"

She doesn't answer and we walk all the way to the stilt houses where she lives with everybody awful quiet. And then she goes inside, and her sister comes with me a little way along the narrow cat walk.

"Oh Tuan, Mu Lan loves you very dearly," she says. "She loves you more than it is good to love anyone, either a man or a woman. She knows how you love Rani. So each night she comes and prays to the Monkey God and asks him what she shall do."

She walks with me a little way farther and her face gets terrible sad. "I have prayed to the Monkey God also, Tuan, for I am greatly troubled. A Chinese girl is not like your girls of the West. The hearts of the Chinese girls are like hidden rivers in the desert which spring up a little way and then vanish again in the sand. We see only that water which runs outside. I have known Mu Lan since I carried her as a baby in my arms; all her life I have been to her as a mother. But the Mu Lan I see now I do not understand. Even I do not know what she will do."

Like I said, the Lord sure ain't planned things right the way they are between men and women; it'd sure be better if people grew in the ground like carrots or on bushes like huckleberries. Sometimes I get to thinking He did it this way on purpose, just to keep men and women praying. Because if people stopped praying to Him about love, there'd be a lot of empty seats in the churches.

Chapter XI

I tried to pay more attention to Mu Lan now, making a little fuss about how good her cooking was, and practicing more mountain songs with her, because I sure didn't want any harm to come to her on account of me. And she seemed to get kind of better for a while.

Once I noticed her studying the back of the mountain song book I gave her that's got a few pages about other mountain things besides songs. And then I see her baking something in the Malay stove, and then she puts it on the table and smiles. And I see it's a pan of steaming hot corn bread she'd learned to make from the book.

It was fine, and I told her so. And she looked real happy.

But she still wasn't anything like the way she used to be before.

Things kept on being quiet with the Harmonious Daggers. I'd see the fellows on the green bicycles racing around town like they were on their way to start some new trouble; but they never come near us and I sure was glad.

At the school things were really humming, and more students kept coming all the time. And with Mr. Bascom teaching the music and everything else, we got bigger and better every day.

He'd even started an American band that people hired for funerals and weddings; we got the instruments cheap one day from a band that was breaking up on a cruise ship. He taught them a few pieces, all of them old-timers, because he didn't know any new tunes; of the ones they played their favorite was *I'm Always Chasing Rainbows.* Course they didn't know what the words meant; so sometimes you'd see them in a funeral playing it and tooting away, right ahead of the coffin.

The Pit game we started was spreading all over town, and some of our graduates opened little places like Bingo parlors, where people could sit down and drink tea and play Pit by the hour. And a couple of times fellows wanted to study in the classes until we told them different; they thought it was a school to make them win at gambling.

And a bunch of girls came over with the lady that ran one of the loveboats; they'd heard about the other lady went to the school, and she was doing so fine now, they wanted to come, too. And I didn't want to hurt their feelings so I told them the classes was full.

Nearly every one of our graduates was becoming a big success. The old fellow that had wanted to get married came in to see me one day, and he looked wonderful. "O Tuan, my relatives no longer send me children's presents," he said. "I have not only one wife, but now I have three. And I also have two concubines."

The little fellow that'd always wanted to be a boxer—his

name was Jemal—was boxing regular now, and doing fine. And he was boxing one of the big fellows in town for a kind of championship and asked me to come and see him fight. It was in a big hall kind of like they have fights in back home, with a platform and ropes in the middle. But the fighting sure ain't the same; they fight with their hands and feet and knees and teeth, and bite and kick every which way.

The fellow Jemal was fighting was a giant Chinese twice as big as him. And when you looked at him standing there almost naked, with his big muscles playing like snakes, you were sure in two seconds Jemal'd look like he'd gone through a sausage grinder. But Jemal keeps out of his way awful smart, and then about half way through lands a wallop on him right in the stomach. And the big Chinese drops to the boards and lays there stone cold while he takes the count; for a couple of minutes he looks like a statue in a cemetery.

I went back to Jemal's dressing room to tell him how great he done.

"I owe it all to the school, Tuan," he says, and he looks around to see if anybody's watching. And then he shows me inside his kind of boxing gloves, and there's a big piece of iron.

I told him that sure wasn't what we were teaching in the school, but I guess he didn't understand. Because he thanked me again and next day he sent me a present of a big box of peanut candy and ginger.

It wasn't long after that and I'm on the boat and I see the lieutenant of police coming.

"Have you seen anything of Mabub Ali?" he says. That was the name of the big Sikh that wanted to be a bank guard.

"I ain't seen him since he graduated," I say. "That was six months ago. Is he looking for a job?"

"We're looking for him," the lieutenant says. "He got the job all right. Being guard for the big Chinese bank. He made a deal with some thieves, and they robbed it last night. Of ten thousand dollars."

Well, like G.B. said, I guess you had to take the bad with the good.

The drought and the heat kept getting worse and worse. And I guess it did something funny to Amok. One afternoon I saw him pick up a knife and give a terrible howl, and start running down the gangplank. And the people that were there on the wharf shouted "Amuck! Amuck!" and started running in every direction. Lucky Mock Duck and Teddy were there and we got him down on the ground, and it took all the three of us could do to hold him. And after a few minutes he stopped thrashing like a lion, and he was all right again.

This time I told him he was fired sure and I told him to pack up and go. I told him I was sorry but I couldn't have him around any more. And he did what I said and left, and then a couple of hours later I looked out and I saw him laying in his little skirt with a bundle of his other clothes right in front of the gangplank; so nobody could keep from stepping on him if they wanted to get on or get off.

I went out and told him to go away, but he only started crying. "O Tuan, I love you," he said. "If you do not let me stay I will lie here without eating or drinking till I die."

So of course I had to take him back.

Well, I was more crazy than ever about Rani. And I'd made up my mind to marry her as soon as I could. I knew that marrying was fine with her. But I'd kind of hinted to her mother a couple of times and I could see the old lady was kind of worried. She went to the Hindu temple all the time and was awful superstitious. And I could tell she was afraid something bad would happen with Rani marrying somebody of a different religion and country like me.

It was sure the funniest kind of going with a girl you ever saw, having her mother tag along every second, and sometimes it drove me kind of crazy. But that was the way of the country, and wasn't anything else you could do.

I still went to the taxi-dance place at the Happy World a couple of times a week. The Happy World was all different now since I'd first been there with Mu Lan. It was all fixed up with our jukeboxes and pin ball machines, just like Coney Island. And I'd buy up most of Rani's tickets for the night. And Rani's mother would sit there watching without saying a word, and the other mothers would be watching, too. And they looked like fat little gods.

Well, things had been awful quiet for a while with the old-timers and the Harmonious Daggers. And then one night I was out at the dance place and the jukebox was going strong and everybody except Rani and me were dancing. And I saw the Tunku's brother come in with the two fellows in the green sarongs, and start looking over the girls again. I hadn't seen him since the time I'd had the row about Rani, but I noticed him and the others looking at me pretty hard, and I guess it must have reminded them about me and what'd happened.

It was maybe four or five nights later, and I was at the Happy World again. Rani had finished work, and she and her mother and Teddy and me were having something to eat in a little Chinese restaurant right next to the place where she danced. The Chinese waiter put the sweet and sour shrimp I'd ordered on the table, and I'd dipped in the ivory chopsticks Teddy'd give me some time before.

I was bringing a shrimp to my mouth when all of a sudden Teddy gives a shout.

"Don't eat it, Tuan!" he cries, and hits my chopsticks so hard with his hand they fly all the way across the floor. And then he runs over and picks up the chopsticks and comes back to the table and holds them out before me.

"Look, Tuan!" he says. And I look, and they're black as the ink the big octopuses there shoot at you in the sea.

"It is poison, Tuan," he says. "That is why I gave you the chopsticks of ivory. Whenever there is poison in what someone gives you to eat it turns the ivory black."

And then he goes over and smells the shrimps and nods his head. "It would have killed you fifty times, Tuan."

And Rani turns pale and reaches out and takes my hand, and her mother just sits shivering.

And then Teddy calls the waiter over, and asks him to bring the owner, and the owner comes, a big heavy-set Chinaman with red eyes like a rat. And Teddy takes the bowl of shrimps and throws it in the owner's face. And then he walks out.

We go toward the gate and even by the moonlight I can see his bald head is purple. "I know who has done this, Tuan," he says. "I will make them very sorry, Tuan."

The drought ended the next week the way it generally does out there, with a big typhoon. We knew it was coming a couple of days ahead—they got the word from Manila—and everybody moved their boats to better places. We put ours in a kind of cove between two hills where everybody said it'd be safer. All the people in the little houses on stilts where Mu Lan lived had to get out, because they said it was going to be flooded. So she and her married sister and Mock Duck packed up and came to stay on the boat. And then they said the Hindu people where Rani lived had to leave, so she and her mother and five of her brothers and sisters came on the boat, too. And Amok brought his wife and their old father and mother, and half a dozen kids. And then Mr. Bascom came and said could he bring Mrs. Kanaka.

"She has no place to go," he told me. "And they say her house will be flooded by two feet of water. It is odd but with my salary from your school I could go to one of the inns again. The noise at Mrs. Kanaka's is frightful and the beetles and the ants are appalling. And because I used to feed the pig when it was very small, sometimes it insists on sleeping with me. But I have formed an attachment to the house, and Mrs. Kanaka makes excellent tea. It all goes to prove as I used to declare in my lectures to the girls at Miss Fairlee's: of all the human factors in our lives the most important is habit."

Course I said Mrs. Kanaka could come, so she arrived a couple of hours later with the seven giggling little girls and the babies and maybe twenty chickens and the two dogs and the pig. And Mr. Bascom came carrying his clothes on hangers and hung them up carefully on nails. He looked at his pants he'd took the crease out of packing, and Mrs. Kanaka saw he was worried. So she put a pair in a chair with a couple of boards on top and then made two of the little girls squeeze into the seat and sit on them without moving.

And then her two dogs came up to our cat, and I thought there was going to be a big fight. But instead the cat started rubbing against them, and the dogs began licking her fur. I guess something told them about the hurricane.

The two dogs began to howl and scratch their sides something awful. And Mr. Bascom sprayed them out of a special can of insecticide and they stopped scratching right away. And then they began licking off the spray just like it was candy. I thought they must be covered with fleas, but I was afraid the insecticide would kill them.

But Mr. Bascom shook his head. "They have not a single flea left," he says. "The scratching and howling are a signal. It is a signal to me they wish more of this insecticide to lick. I think it tends to prove my theory; habit is as important to animals as it is to humans. This is an acquired taste, as babies cry for soothing syrup."

And then the cat began licking them, too. I tell you we sure had a houseful.

Well, a typhoon ain't much fun. Though I was glad of it one way; it gave me a chance to have Rani near me every minute.

It started kind of quiet, with a gray sky and some thin clouds sweeping past, like the smoke when you burn leaves back home in the fall. And then the smoke got thicker, and the wind began to blow a little, and a few drops of rain fell. And then the clouds got black and the wind kept getting stronger and stronger. And pretty soon the rain came and it wasn't like any rain you ever saw before. When you looked out the window it was just like you were in a glass bowl dropped down to the bottom of the ocean. There wasn't anything in the world around you but water.

The wind got shriller and shriller, and began screeching like a million busted train whistles were blowing on top of the roof. And the glass in the windows began to kind of bend, till it looked like they were made of rubber. All of a sudden there was a terrific roar and the whole tin roof of the boat came off; and I saw it go rolling onto the land, just like it was a roll of carpet. And Rani and her mother and the rest of her family put out the little gods they'd brought, and dropped to their knees and began to pray. And I go over and put my hand on her shoulder and tell her not to worry.

Amok's kids sat by him awful still and quiet; and the seven little girls snuggled around Mrs. Kanaka, like seven little mice. And the pig and the two dogs and the cat all tried to crowd together under a little cabinet, in a space not big enough if they were ants.

With the tin gone water began to pour in from the ceiling in maybe a hundred places. And I went around putting out pots and pans and throwing down pieces of carpet.

Mu Lan looked kind of solemn, but she wasn't scared like the others.

"I will help you, Tuan," she said.

She searched in the kitchen and put out more of the

pans. And the drops of water hitting the tin were like a 100-piece orchestra.

The boat began to rock like it was a teeter-totter. And the chairs and tables slid around like they were on roller skates. And you had to hang on to something like glue or you'd be knocked to the floor.

Rani and her family prayed harder. And her mother said the gods were angry because of the atomic bombs and were going to destroy the world.

The teeter-tottering stopped for a while and the boat got quiet.

"I was in a typhoon in New Orleans once," Mr. Bascom said. "We call it a hurricane there. We were all assembled in a schoolhouse like this, for there was fear a levee would break and the district where I lived would be inundated. We all played charades, where one acts out a historic or well known scene and the others must guess the scene one is portraying. My group chose George Washington crossing the Delaware and the younger Washington throwing a stone across the same river. I played the older Washington and the younger one as well. This was very appropriate because my family in Charleston, the Dinwiddies, were related to General Washington."

I could see him thinking a minute. "Perhaps we could play the charades now," he says. "I think it might improve our spirits."

And he folds his arms and scowls and gives a couple of military commands and paces back and forth. And he scowls again, and then he imitates a bugle blowing the charge.

And then he smiles and asks us what he's acting. Nobody knows and he looks disappointed.

"It is Napoleon before Waterloo," he says. "Planning his campaign."

He starts another one and imitates a band playing *The*

Star-Spangled Banner. And you hear a bugle again and he comes in and salutes very happy. And then he goes to the other side of the room and acts out somebody else coming and the new fellow salutes very solemn. And then the first fellow sits down at a table and signs a paper and the solemn fellow signs the paper, too. And the solemn fellow looks awful sad and takes a stick and hands it across the table. But the happy fellow smiles and shakes his head and gives the solemn man the stick back. And then they both smile, and shake hands, and the band plays *Star-Spangled Banner* again and then *Dixie*.

This time nobody knows what he's acting, the same as before.

"It is the signing of the treaty at Appomattox in the War Between The States," he says. "With General Grant returning the sword of General Robert E. Lee."

He started to act out a couple more, but the boat began to teeter again, and it knocked the breath right out of you. So he gave up trying.

Night came and the storm got even worse, though the rocking stopped a little. Mu Lan helped me get out some sandwiches and things and Mrs. Kanaka managed to make some tea. And Rani and the others drank a little, and went back to praying. And every once in a while I'd go up to Rani and give her a pat on the shoulder again. And she'd look at me kind of childish and worried, like a little girl I seen once in Muleshoe that belonged to a family that was driving through and she got lost some way from the car and I stayed with her till the family came back.

Well, the storm kept up most of the night, and then I guess about three in the morning the eye arrived. And the stars came out so bright they looked like colored lights on a Christmas tree. And then the storm hit again, and then around noon it ended. And Rani and her family and Mr. Bascom and the others thanked me, and they went on home. And Mu Lan and Mock Duck and Amok and me started to clean up.

We weren't too bad off, just the tin roof gone and a few of the windows cracked. But when I went around town to look, Menang was sure a mess. Thatched roofs blown down from the native houses everywhere, and coconut trees pulled up by the roots and laying on the ground like dead people.

I was on the way back to the boat when I saw everybody kind of running around awful scared, like when there's a big fire or something.

I stopped at the Four Elephants to find out how Bertie and Alf had got on. And I saw the place was still all boarded up; they hadn't come back yet from the high ground where they were living. But the little Malay was there who took care of the place, and he rushed up to me.

"O Tuan, have you heard?" he asked. "Something terrible has happened. In the typhoon all the sacred snakes have left the snake temple. First the typhoon and now the snakes. It is a sign the gods are very angry at the people of Menang. It is a sign they will destroy the city."

An old shriveled Chinese standing nearby nodded. "Once before the snakes left, that was a hundred years ago in the time of my father's father. And a great plague came and over half the people in Menang died. If I had the money like you, Tuan, I would take a boat, and go far from here, to Hong Kong. For a grave evil is certain to come, Tuan."

It got worse and worse, and what they call panic spread everywhere, like when I was a boy back at Muleshoe, and the big flu epidemic came and everybody was dying.

I hired some men to nail the tin roof back on, but they didn't work at all.

"O Tuan, it is hard to work when tomorrow we may all be dead," said a Chinese heating tar. "They say that last night the volcano threw up great flaming stones as large as a house, and a voice called out of the flames like thunder. They say the volcano will blow up and all Menang will sink into the sea."

I was surprised that afternoon when the police came down to the boat, and looked it over from end to end; but they didn't say what they were wanting.

I'd noticed Teddy had a queer look in his scarecrow eyes for several days, and that night after everybody's gone, he takes me by the arm.

"Come Tuan," he says, and he takes a flashlight and pulls up a hatch cover, and we go down into the hull. It's terribly damp and smelly there, and I see some big rats go running past. And we keep on moving to the bow, and he pulls off some boards look like they're nailed tight, and I see a big wooden box. And he opens the lid a crack and I hear a terrible hissing. And he opens it a little more and I see snakes' heads darting around, with their tongues flickering like forked lightning. And I know without his saying a word; they're the sacred snakes from the big snake temple.

Teddy looks at them proudly. "This is to pay for the poison they put in your shrimps, Tuan. I stole the snakes when all the priests were busy with the typhoon. What do you wish me to do with them, Tuan?"

I'm so shocked I can hardly talk. "You've got to give 'em back," I say.

He looks hurt. "I cannot do this which you ask, Tuan. The temple is the sacred temple of the Tunku and the Harmonious Daggers and the snakes are its holy gods. With the snakes away the chief priest has lost terrible face. He must clothe himself in sackcloth and bow his head in shame. And the Tunku's brother and the Harmonious Daggers must do the same."

"You've got to get them off the boat, anyway. This minute," I say.

He looks worse hurt than ever. "O Tuan, it is such a

beautiful place for them to hide. And the rats make their stay here a pleasure."

He closes the box again. "The police are watching my poor house as a starving hawk watches a hare. And they have already been here on the boat, so they will not come again. Please, Tuan, let them stay."

"Get 'em off quick," I say.

And he takes the box, and puts it on his skinny back. And I go off to bed.

About four or five days later I hear a noise in the middle of the night, and I jump up, not knowing what was wrong. And I go out on deck, and there's Teddy carrying the box of snakes again. I was kind of wild.

"I told you I didn't want 'em on the boat," I said. "What do you mean by bringing 'em here now?"

"O Tuan, I am not bringing them," he says. "I am taking them away."

"But I saw you taking them once," I answer.

"Yes, Tuan. I took them away as you commanded. But you did not say I could not bring them back. And there was no other place for them to hide."

"Where are you taking 'em now?" I ask.

A funny little smile goes across his yellow face. "I am taking them to the priest at the snake temple, Tuan. He and the Tunku's brother have paid the Celestial Tigers much money."

The temple had a big celebration when the snakes came back. The head priest said the snakes had gone to Heaven to be with the gods there and now they'd be wiser and holier than ever.

A couple of weeks after that I had to pay the bill for the roof. It was pretty high, and though everything was going fine, I was telling Mr. Bascom I was a little short of ready cash.

Teddy heard me talking and came to me a few minutes

later. "O Tuan, I will get you this money," he says. "I will kidnap someone. There are many rich men in Menang who have not yet been kidnaped. And it is much easier to kidnap a man than a snake."

I told him I figured I'd get along. I guess you can't beat a Chinaman.

One good thing the typhoon did, it smashed up the club-house of the Harmonious Daggers pretty bad, and I knew they'd be busy fixing it up for a while. And then Teddy took two more societies into the Celestial Tigers, the Seven Crescent Moons Society and the Society of the Ghostly Mountain, and he was really getting big now.

And it looked like nobody was going to bother us any more; they were too afraid of Teddy.

Chapter XII

About this time Tai Pusam came
along, that's the big Hindu holiday of the year. Rani and
her mother always went to the big Hindu temple near the
boat, and a couple of times I went with them. It was full of
incense, with those funny gods and goddesses standing all
around have maybe sixteen arms and legs; they look like an
octopus that's got the itch and is trying to scratch all its legs
at once.

Rani was going to be in the procession they have that
day, so I went with Mr. Bascom and Teddy to watch. There
were thousands of Hindus marching in all kinds of queer
costumes; and then come a cart drawn by two sacred cows
dressed up with wreaths and strings of beautiful flowers.
And behind the cart came the people carrying the kedavi,
that's a kind of heavy wooden frame like I seen once in a

wax torture museum, a thousand awful looking spikes that press down like needles into you. Rani's uncle was carrying one this year—it's a big honor they say; and Rani and all his relatives were marching beside him, kind of encouraging him as he walked along, because those spikes must have felt pretty terrible. She was dressed like the others, in a robe white as snow, and her head was bowed low, praying.

"She is truly beautiful," said Mr. Bascom. "She looks like an angel walking in a procession of the saints in Heaven."

Well, the parade comes to an open place where they'd built a big fire with a lot of red hot coals, and then a lot of drums and flutes begin to play. And Rani's uncle and the others carrying the kedavis lay them on the ground; and they go up to the coals, and start chanting a strange kind of song, and begin walking across. And queer thing, it looks like it don't hurt them any more than if they're walking over a red carpet.

And then the other people begin crossing over, and I see Rani getting ready, too. And I get all shivery inside, because I'd heard that sometimes they get burned bad. And it'd be terrible if a beautiful girl like that got even a little mark on her.

"Don't do it, Rani!" I call. But in the noise of the chanting and the drums and the flutes, she doesn't hear a word. And I start to run toward her, but Teddy holds me back.

"Do not stop her, Tuan," he says. "It might bring her great evil. It might even cause her to burn to death."

Course I know he was right. It was because I loved her so much that I'd even spoke.

The drums beat like thunder and the flutes play like crazy people screaming, and she puts one foot in the fire. And she takes a step and another and another, and I watch like I'm turned to dry ice. She walks step after step, awful slow, like the queen in a fairy comic I read once, coming out of the fire that some witches had started to kill her. And pretty

THE SIGN OF THE PRAYING TIGER

soon she was safe on the other side, and I run up to her.

"Are you all right, Rani?" I ask.

She looks at me for a couple of seconds as if she doesn't know me. "I am all right, Tuan," she says in a far-off voice, and then the kind of veil I seen sometimes comes over her eyes and her family takes her away.

Your brain's sure a queer thing. In the back of the dictionary, after the Wisdom of the World and Weights and Measures there was some pages, Science in a Nutshell, and it said with all man's inventions there ain't no machine to equal the human brain. And I figure that's sure right. Way it seems to me your brain's like you put a lot of numbers in one of them little gambling cages they use to play Bingo, and spin them around, and you never know what number's coming out. A couple of days after the fire walking I got a letter from Muleshoe saying how a girl I grew up with there had been made Miss Kentucky in the Miss America contest. And that made me look at the picture of Miss America we had up on the wall wearing her fancy white dress and gold crown, and saying "This Could Be You."

And I'd never thought of it before, but now instead of the girl in that picture from Enid, Oklahoma, or wherever it was, all I could see now was Rani in her white dress, looking like an angel, ready to walk through the fire.

"I'll bet if she was back home she'd be Miss America," I say to Mr. Bascom.

He nods. "As I told you, I once had the pleasure of seeing Miss America in person. When I was staying with my sister in her cottage at Lake Pontchartrain. I spoke with her for some moments at the clubhouse where my sister was entertaining some ladies from Richmond, in Virginia. I wished to discuss with her the interesting ideas about physical culture held by the ancient Greeks, that linked the beauty of the body with the beauty of the mind. But she said she was sorry, the only Greek she knew had a popcorn stand in her hometown somewhere in the Middle West—I cannot quite remember the state. I believe it was Ohio or Illinois, or perhaps it was California."

And then the numbers in the gambling cage spun again, and I got another idea.

"Why don't we have a beauty contest here?" I said. "It'll be fine advertising for the school and for the town besides. We'll get the merchants and the teahouses to give some good prizes, and we'll pick out the prettiest girl and make her Miss Menang."

Mr. Bascom's face lighted. "I witnessed a beauty contest in New Orleans once," he said. "It was given by the merchants in the neighborhood where I resided."

He looked kind of regretful for a minute. "The butcher where I bought my meat had asked me to be a judge because of my connection with Miss Fairlee's. But the board of Miss Fairlee's decided it would not accord with the dignity of the school. So I was compelled to decline."

The seven little girls of Mrs. Kanaka had come down to the boat and were watching a lemonade seller on the wharf. They caught Mr. Bascom's eye, and he called the lemonade man over.

The girls each had a drink and Mr. Bascom got ready to pay. And I noticed something I'd never noticed before, he was carrying three little pocketbooks in his coat, one holding Menang pennies and the others nickels and dimes.

"I find the three purses very convenient," he explained. "Now that my income is so much improved, with the coins separated in this way I can always pay with the exact change. It prevents my being cheated and besides saves considerable time."

But I noticed when he paid it took him twice as long as anybody else. The three pocketbooks were exactly alike and he opened and shut each one a couple of times to look inside; he couldn't tell which pocketbook was which.

Well, everybody thought the beauty contest was a fine idea. And I talked to the merchants and the teahouses and they said O.K. so we got to work right away. We decided we'd do it just like they do in the States, and have it go by what they call elimination. First, we'd give a prize for the prettiest Malay girl and the prettiest Chinese and Hindu and the prettiest girl that was half-caste. And then we'd pick out the prettiest of the four, and she'd be Miss Men-ang, and the queen of everything that went on for the rest of the year. And like back home it wouldn't be just for looks. They'd all have to do something besides being pretty, like dancing or singing, or maybe making a speech.

I tell you there was plenty of excitement in the town when the people heard; there hadn't been anything like it on the island ever before. They'd seen American beauty contests in the films, and all the girls wanted to win. And everywhere you'd go you'd see the girls making new dresses, or maybe singing a Chinese song, or practicing a new Malay or American dance.

"It reminds me of New Orleans," Mr. Bascom said. "At the time of the Mardi Gras. Before they have chosen the Queen."

Course Rani entered right away, and all the girls at the school. At first Mu Lan said she wouldn't go in; she was so terribly shy. But I and all the others told her how pretty she was, so she finally gave me one of her old-time smiles and said she would. And looked like everybody was happy, except of course the priests and the old-timers. They said it was defiling the religion and girls ought to stay at home. And they began making all kinds of threats again, but we didn't pay too much attention.

I thought a couple of times my ivory chopsticks got black again, but turned out it was just bad cooking, not poison. And a couple of times I was sure I heard a mob coming again, but turned out it was another Chinese or Malay holiday, and people were just celebrating. And once I saw two of the green bicycles stop in front of the wharf again, and I thought everything was starting all over. But turned out one of them had a flat, and they'd stopped to fix the tire.

For maybe a couple of weeks we had what they call the preliminaries, the same as they call them in boxing; choosing the prettiest girls in each of the four different kinds of people, the Malays and the Chinese and the Hindus and the half-castes, in each of the four different parts of Menang. These were the river and the ocean and the mountain districts, and the district that was the middle of town.

There'd be trouble sometimes when one girl would win and the relatives and friends of the losers got mad. And sometimes after the contests you'd see the mothers start arguing; and then maybe there'd be some hair-pulling and fighting, and then the girls' fathers and brothers'd join in, and sometimes the girls themselves. I was kind of surprised, because I'd never heard of anything like that with a beauty contest in the States. But it didn't do too much harm cause nobody got really hurt bad.

Well, the big day came at last, and people began gathering on the bank right after the sun was up. And wasn't long before the girls started coming on the boat with their mothers, and they looked so beautiful in their fancy dresses it almost hurt your eyes. We didn't have them in bathing suits, because we knew they wouldn't have worn them; if they had we knew the old-timers would have started shooting right away. There were sixteen girls, four from each of the four districts like I said, out of maybe four or five hundred that had tried. Course Rani and Mu Lan both were there, Rani with three other half-caste girls, and Mu Lan with the Chinese. There hadn't ever been any doubt about them two; they had both won in a walk.

By eleven o'clock, when the contest was to start, the wharf and the street in back of it were jammed; everybody

in Menang was there that could hobble or walk. We had
the boat fixed up with flags and bunting and things till you
couldn't see a piece of wood hardly, with benches for the
big people in the town, the planters, and the big merchants,
and a bench for the judges, too. I went around, talking to
the judges and the girls, and made sure everything was all
ready.

The chief judge was Mr. Bascom and he was wearing
what he called a morning coat with a white flower bigger
than ever. And he was hopping around so excited and gay,
he looked like a cottontail rabbit just come out of his bur-
row in the spring. And there were four other judges, all big
people in the town, a Malay and a Chinese and a half-caste,
and one that was a Hindu.

The Malay girls were to open the contest and I gave the
signal for the first one to come up on the platform. And I
saw her start and I motioned the band to begin. They were
supposed to play a waltz, but with Mr. Bascom being a
judge, some Chinese fellow was acting as the leader. And
they'd just got a new book of band music from Singapore,
and they'd learned a new piece they thought was pretty.
And they began to play, and it was a funeral march. I didn't
stop them because I was afraid it might make the Malay girl
nervous; I knew she didn't have any idea what it was so it
wouldn't make any difference.

This girl did a dance with a kris, jabbing and stabbing
everywhere until you thought she'd kill herself; it kind of
made your hair curl. And another did a puppet dance and
one played the gongs and one did what they call a shadow
show. They were each allowed five minutes, and every once
in a while one of the mothers of the girls would run up on
the platform where her daughter was performing and right
in the middle straighten a wrinkle in her dress or put down a
couple of stray hairs.

They finished, and the judges talked a minute, and then

they picked the girl that played the gongs. And I read off her name, and Mr. Bascom put a little silver crown on her head, and gave her a silver loving cup, and she was Miss Malay Menang.

And there was some clapping, but there were some boos, too, from the friends of the girls that had lost.

The next were the Hindu girls and two of them did dances and songs playing cymbals and castanets. And one did a dance with a snake and one did a dance through a hoop of fire. The judges picked the one with the snake, a girl with big dark eyes, like saucers of black china. And Mr. Bascom crowned her and gave her a cup like the other. And she was Miss Hindu Menang.

This time there were a lot of boos, and I saw the Hindu people get all excited. And some of them hurried up to the judges, and the judges began to whisper. Pretty soon there's a big crowd of Hindus around Miss Hindu Menang, arguing and chattering like squirrels over a bag of peanuts. And then the judges come up, too, and everybody starts shouting and shaking their fists. And then Mr. Bascom comes running over to me, and I ask him what's the matter.

"They say we have made a dreadful mistake," he says. "They say she is not a Hindu girl at all. She is an Egyptian girl off a loveboat."

Well, it turns out it's true. And the Egyptian and the Hindu girls start fighting. And we make them stop, and a couple of the big judges from Menang take the crown and the cup away, though they had a hard time getting them; the girl bit and scratched like a wildcat, and the snake was pretty nasty. And the judges talk again and they give the Hindu crown to the girl that danced through the hoop of fire.

This time some friends of the Egyptian girl boo and holler to get new judges. And the mothers of the other girls that lost and their friends start booing, too.

And then things calm down and it's time for the Chinese. The first Chinese girl did a dance with a kind of bells, and the next recited a Chinese poem, and the next started a kind of tumbling act. She had a head looked just like her own tied behind her, right where she sat down. And when she'd start tumbling you couldn't tell which head you were seeing, because she looked exactly the same when she was upside down.

And she's right in the middle when a bunch of fat Chinese women come running up to the judges, and start arguing and waving their hands. And the girl doing the tumbling act stops, and there's a big row again.

And Mr. Bascom comes over and he's all upset. "They say she has been married," he tells me. "In that case of course, it is a gross deception. There was a similar grave error at home not long before I left. But fortunately it was discovered before it became too late. A girl was about to be crowned Miss New Orleans. And the judges learned she was the mother of eleven children and had been married three times."

Well, the tumbling girl and her mother insisted she hadn't been married, and the mothers of the other two Chinese girls and their friends insisted she had. And then it turns out she'd been promised by her father to the son of his best friend, and the son died, and then the way they do sometimes, they married her to his ghost. And the judges talk it over a few minutes, and then said things being the way they were, she could stay on in the contest. So she stepped up on the platform again and went on with her act where she left off.

And then Mu Lan comes out, and you knew in a second who was going to win, she was so much prettier and smarter. And her sister runs up and gives her hair a pat like the mothers had done their daughters before. And then she plays the zither and sings the Chinese song about the girl that loved the pottery maker. And she was so pretty, just like a doll, and her voice sounded so sweet, when she finished everybody stamped on the floor the way they do there and clapped their hands off. And in a minute the judges give me the name of the winner. And I read it slow, "Miss Mu Lan is Miss Chinese Menang."

And then Mr. Bascom comes forward and puts a little silver crown on her head, like he did the other girls, and gives her a silver cup. And everybody clapped again and this time nobody booed. And Mu Lan looked awful happy, the first time I'd seen her that way in weeks. And it sure made me feel good.

And then it was the turn of the half-castes. And they were so beautiful it was hard to believe they were real. And the first one of them starts to play a kind of mandolin they call a lute. And then a little old man with a beard rushes up. "I'm her father!" he yells. "I don't want my daughter here shaming Allah!"

And he grabs her by the arm and tries to pull her off the platform. And her mother rushes up, and screams at the old man, and tries to pull him off their daughter.

Well, we get them separated and the mother shows him some of the prizes the daughter'd have if she wins the crown, and right away he gets quiet. And the girl goes on after that, playing the lute and singing. And then two more half-caste girls play Hindu and Malay tunes, and dance kind of slow and solemn.

And then Rani comes out all in silver and does a dance like she was one of the Hindu idols with the sixteen arms and legs trying to scratch themselves like the octopus. Only she is all covered with bracelets and whichever way she moves she tinkles like temple bells. And it was wonderful what she did with her hands; her fingers were always flashing and pointing. You could tell they were saying different things, even if you didn't know the meaning; it was like somebody talking to you deaf and dumb when you didn't understand the language. And all the big people on the benches clap even harder than for Mu Lan. And I read out the slip the judges give me, "Miss Rani is Miss Mixed Men-ang." And Mr. Bascom puts a silver crown on her head and gives her a silver cup, too. And this time like it was with Mu Lan, there wasn't a single boo.

Chapter XIII

We stopped for lunch now and we gave the big people on the benches some fine Chinese food; we wanted to do things in style.

Teddy came up to me while they were eating and pointed off to a white-bearded old Chinaman wearing fancy clothes. With the old fellow were two little boys dressed up like princes.

I could see Teddy's all excited. "That is the richest man in Menang, Tuan," he says. "And those are his two favorite grandchildren. Let me kidnap all three, will you, Tuan? They never go out from their home, and in their house they are surrounded by many fences of electric wires and the most terrible dogs on the island. And I have heard there is even a black, full-grown leopard. It is a wonderful chance, Tuan."

Course I told him he was crazy.

There was a lot of booing in the crowd now, especially from young fellows I guess were friends of the girls that had lost the contests today and the contests held in the districts. And some of them yelled to get new judges, too. And Mr. Bascom and the other judges began to get kind of worried. And the rest of the people yelled to them to be quiet, and there were a few fights.

And then lunch is over, and the merchants bring up all the prizes and put them in a big pile; rugs and beautiful silks, and jewelry, and Chinese pottery and chairs.

Alf had come over from the bar to watch because he knew there wouldn't be any business. "Whoever wins all those bloody prizes is going to be a bloody rich girl," he rumbles. "She won't have to do any more work the rest of her life."

Well, the band started playing, the right piece this time, and the show started again. And then the Malay girl that played the gongs comes out, and this time she plays a saxophone. And then the Hindu girl that danced through the hoop walks onto the platform all covered with jewels, and does what they call the jewel dance. And she throws the jewels all around—I guess they're colored glass. And then Mu Lan comes on, and this time she's dressed like the Kentucky Mountain girl the night we had the first dance. And she sings *On Top of Old Smoky* the same as she'd done before, only this time it was a million times better. And the people clapped and stamped their feet till I thought the floor'd fall in.

And then Rani came out, and this time she was dressed all in gold, wearing a crown like a queen. And in one hand she was carrying two masks, one of a king, and one of some kind of knight. And she began to act out a story, with nothing except her face and the masks and her hands. It was a story about how the king, her husband, gets jealous because of the knight that's a friend, though the king ain't got any reason. I seen some pretty fine acting in the picture shows, but I never seen anything like that before. You could see everything those three people done, even what they were thinking. And in the end when the king stabs her and she falls to the floor dead, you feel so bad you wished you had a knife to kill him, too. And then the friend comes in and finds her body and he stands there all choked up. And he takes his sword and kills the king, and then he kills himself. Though of course there wasn't any man there at all, only a couple of paper masks.

Well, the people clapped and roared; they made so much noise if the volcano had blowed up right then nobody would have noticed.

And then all four of the girls walk up and down before the judges a couple of times, and everybody gets quiet. And the judges lean their heads close together and they all start whispering. And then Mr. Bascom gives me a paper and I read out slow: "Miss Rani is Miss Menang."

And pretty near everybody starts clapping again and Rani goes kind of white. And her family rush up and give her a hug. And Mu Lan and the Hindu and the Malay girl do the same like they've watched the American girls in the movies. But I can see Mu Lan's got tears in her eyes. And the band gets excited and mixed up again and starts playing the funeral march. And three little girls come out holding a tray with a big golden crown. And they bring it up to Mr. Bascom, and he puts it on Rani's head.

"I crown you Miss Menang," he says. "A true queen of grace and beauty."

And I go up to her and she talks to me low, and says, "Thank you, Tuan." And she gives me a soft loving look, and I'm so proud I wouldn't have traded places with George Washington the day he became President.

And then I see Mu Lan going off with her sister, and I see

her eyes are full of tears now that she won't let come down. And I try to say something to her but she hurries away. And I sure feel sorry.

And then a lot of the Chinese and Hindu and Malay people get mad, now their girls have lost; and they start booing and hissing though most of them hadn't booed at all before. I guess they'd had time to think.

Some of them call the judges nasty names and there were arguments and little fights everywhere; and this time the judges looked really scared. And they talked low to each other, and then Mr. Bascom came over.

"They say they would like escorts," he told me. "They say they are afraid to go home alone."

I asked Teddy to take them and he looked kind of miserable.

"I will do this because you ask it, Tuan," he said. "But these are very rich men. I would be much happier if instead of guarding, you would ask me to kidnap them."

And then I saw his scarecrow face brighten. "Perhaps they will invite me into their homes for a cup of tea," he says. "In that case it will be very good. For then I can see where they keep their dogs and the switches that control the electric fences outside."

He goes off with them and they don't seem very happy, because of course they know who he is. With the skinny Teddy walking kind of nervous at their heels, they look just like fat young lambs being guarded by a hungry wolf.

"You've done something I'd have said wasn't bloody possible," Alf tells me, mopping his big red face with a bandana as he starts off to the bar. "These women in Menang were always sweet and timid as bloody mice, never even raising their voices. And today I seen 'em screaming and howling and clawing each other to pieces. I guess if you tell even a lady mouse she or her daughter ain't as pretty as another mouse, it's like she's swallowed something that turns her into a bloody wildcat."

For a little while it looks like there's going to be bad trouble. And then everybody goes home. But in a few days everything's all quieted down, and everybody says it was a wonderful contest, and asking when we'll have the next one.

That night for the first time I had dinner in Rani's house with her family at a big celebration. And the place is full of the carpets and silks and all the prizes she's won, and everybody's terrible happy. And nobody says anything, but I can tell now they're expecting us to marry.

The next two days Mu Lan didn't come to the boat at all—that was the first time she'd missed since I'd been in Menang. And when she came the morning of the third day she sure looked terrible. She didn't cry or anything; just went around like a ghost.

I could see Mock Duck was awful worried. He was all jumpy and uneasy, like a old raccoon in winter when the ground's covered with snow and there ain't any food around. He put the Kitchen God out in the sun again, and wouldn't give him the betel nut or even a grain of rice. I didn't know whether Mu Lan was that way because she'd lost the contest; or whether it was because she'd seen the look that Rani gave me. Or maybe she'd heard about my going to her house that night for supper, and maybe knowing how among the Hindu people that meant something special.

I'd just got up, ain't quite a week later, and I was having my shave, when I hear quick little footsteps on the plank. And I look out the window and there's Mu Lan's chubby sister, hurrying as fast as she can, and Mock Duck's a little way behind her. She's not giggling this time, and she's all out of breath, and Mock Duck's the same way. I ask the sister what's the matter.

"O Tuan, it is Mu Lan," she says. "Last night before she went to bed she embraced me and my father, and it was as a person very ill embraces a loved one before he dies. And this morning after she dressed she did not eat, but instead started toward the door. I was surprised and I asked her where she was going.

" 'I am going for a long walk, sister,' she said. 'A walk in a place I have never walked before.'

"And she went outside.

"I was worried and I followed quickly and soon I saw where she was bound; it was the square where the autobus waits that takes pleasure seekers to the volcano. But her face was not of one who seeks pleasure, Tuan. It was the face of the others who go there; the girls who like the Japanese throw themselves into the crater because of unrequited love. This will be my sister's walk."

She stopped for breath. "I know this is true, Tuan. For I have seen her go to the flower seller there and buy a white chrysanthemum. This is what these unhappy pilgrims always do; it is a sign of sacrifice."

"What time does the bus go?" I ask, jerking out my watch.

"It is leaving now, Tuan," she answers. "It will be at the volcano in an hour."

There wasn't a second to lose, so I rushed off with them to a place where I knew we could get a car and drove off to the square. The bus was gone, and we started after it, but it was terribly slow going. The road was narrow, and was crowded with carts and donkeys like it was when Mu Lan and I had done it before, only this time it was some kind of holiday, I don't know what, so it was worse than ever. And then there was a accident when a donkey cart had broken down and blocked everything, and held us up bad.

We finally got through, and came to the volcano and saw the bus standing there empty with some other buses that had come from other parts of the island for the holiday.

A lot of people were climbing the path going to the top of the volcano and I rush up to the driver of the bus I know Mu Lan took and ask him how long he's been there.

"O Tuan, I do not know," he says. "The head of the company which owns this bus is a very stingy man, and does not pay me enough to buy a watch. Maybe it is fifteen minutes. Maybe it is half an hour."

And my heart sinks because it don't take very long to climb up.

I don't wait for Mu Lan's sister and Mock Duck, because I know they couldn't keep up with me, and I start climbing as fast as I can. It's a awful narrow path, sometimes just cinders, and sometimes cut through what they call lava rock, wide enough most times for only one person. Like I said there were a terrible lot of people for the holiday, and I sure wasn't very polite, squeezing and pushing everybody to one side to get past. They looked at me like I was crazy.

The ground's all black and your shoes make a lot of noise on the cinders and lava. And every once in a while you see a puff of smoke above you coming out the crater, and you get a terrible smell of sulphur. And I think of the trip I made with Mu Lan when I first came, and how different this trip is now.

I was almost to the top when I finally thought I saw her up ahead, wearing a plain blue dress, that's a color of mourning in China.

"Mu Lan!" I called.

But she didn't turn around or anything, and I figured maybe I was wrong or maybe she didn't hear me. I was climbing and running and pushing like I was really crazy now. I get closer, and then I can see it's her for certain, walking like a zombie.

"Mu Lan!" I call again.

This time she turns around. And I can see she's wearing

the white chrysanthemum, like her sister said. She stands there a minute like she's hypnotized, with her body all stiff and her face all stony; she's like the people in the temple the night I saw the kuntaow.

And then she turns and starts going on again like she's a machine. She gets to the top, and starts moving across the flat place, all black with cinders, that goes to the edge of the crater. And I'm not far behind.

You can see the center of the volcano plain down below you now, smoking kind of smudgy, like when you're having trouble starting a fire. And the smell of sulphur is so strong around you it hurts your nose, like when you break a bottle of ammonia. Last time we'd been there the volcano was all red and shooting up flames and hot coals; but this time it's all gray and black, like a fire that you've covered with ashes. But you can see it all bubbling underneath, and every once in a while it throws up some gray rocks, like you were watching a geyser.

Mu Lan reaches the edge and stands there, all glassy-eyed, looking down into the crater. And I can tell she's getting ready to jump. And I race down and grab her, and pull her back on the path. She doesn't struggle or anything; she just gives a little kind of gasp, and then she goes all limp. And I hold her a minute and then her eyes open again, and they aren't glassy any more. And then I wait with her till her sister and Mock Duck come. There's a little teahouse near the crater, with a lot of people sitting around at the tables eating. And we walk over there, and I get her some tea, and we sit there drinking quiet. And then we walk down the volcano again, with nobody saying a word.

We get down to the bottom, and she sees the car standing there, and we start walking toward it.

"I am a foolish girl," she says, and nobody talked about it any more.

I go back to the boat, and after dark have a little supper

by myself. And I go to bed early; because I don't feel like talking. And I hear the Chinese girls on the loveboats singing in the distance. And I think how being here is just like when I was a kid laying in bed in the cabin, and I'd look at the firelight hitting the Chinese plates Ma had, and I'd dream how those Chinese people were living.

The way things were going here in Menang, sometimes it was hard to tell whether I was living or dreaming.

Chapter XIV

For a week, I guess, my clothes smelled
of sulphur. And every time I smelled it, I thought of Mu
Lan up there on top of that crater. And I thought about it
long after that, too.

Mu Lan was better now. Seemed like that going up the
volcano did something to her. She was still pretty quiet. But
she'd talk to you now, even though she didn't smile too
much; and she'd stopped going around like a ghost.

But funny thing about Rani. Right after the beauty contest, I noticed she seemed to be kind of changing. People
were paying more attention to her, I guess. The big people
in town that'd been sitting on the benches and saw her,
were asking her to their houses now. There was a rich
Frenchman owned a big rubber plantation outside of town
especially began taking her around; and a couple of times

when I wanted to see her, she was going out with him, and I couldn't. We had a couple of bad arguments, and the kind of veil would come over her eyes and her face would get like a mask; and each time we made up and the mask would go away, and everything was all right again. But when we were quarreling that way sometimes I sure wished I hadn't started the contest.

I noticed she wasn't using the sewing machine much, and one day I saw it was gone. And when I asked her where it was, the little veil started to come over her eyes.

"I sold it, Tuan," she said. "And I have bought a new dress in the Chinese store where the wives of the rich planters go. The wives have told me it is not fashionable for a lady like me to sew her own clothes."

I thought she might have asked me before she sold it. But I didn't say anything. I didn't want to see the mask come again.

Around this time I got a bad scare about the Harmonious Daggers again. I was asleep, and having a nightmare that I was in a jungle along a river somewhere, and all of a sudden a big crocodile jumps out of the water and comes running after me. And I wake up and click on my flashlight that's always by my pillow and I see now it ain't a dream; there's a big lizard on my bed, maybe three feet long, with a kind of purple head and yellow throat, and a body all covered like a rainbow.

And his red eyes are looking at me all wild, and his forked tongue's flashing like fire. And I know right away what it is; it's what they call the Menang Devil, that's more poison than the Gila Monster out in Arizona. He ain't like most lizards that always run off; this kind likes to attack. And I watch him there a minute, panting away, and I know if I'm going to stay alive I have to act fast. Lucky it was a cool night, and I have a thin blanket on me; and I throw it over him and catch him up, the way I did catching snakes sometimes when I was a kid. He struggles like he was a crocodile sure enough, but course he can't see, and I toss blanket and all out the window. And then I hear a splash and I know he's hit the water.

A while before, when I got worried about the Daggers I'd put a kind of gate at the end of the plank, with a strong brass padlock. And I go to look with the flashlight to see if the lock'd been forced.

There were some scratches around the keyhole, but I might have done that myself. I started to go inside again, when I thought I saw one of the green bicycles go riding off in the dark. But a cloud was drifting over the moon and it might have been just a shadow. So I couldn't be sure whether the Menang Devil had come from the Harmonious Daggers, or had just crawled onto the boat some way.

For a day or so after that I thought of getting a dog again, but somehow I didn't.

Everything with the school, though, kept doing fine, and so did Mr. Bascom. Funny thing, I saw him spray a spider one day, and instead of kind of shivering as he used to do, I saw him pick it up after it had stopped moving and wrap it in a piece of tissue paper.

"I chanced to talk with a passenger off a cruise boat," he said. "He is a professor of biology at one of our leading universities. He saw me spraying a beetle as is my custom and when he found I was an educator like himself he asked me if I would send him some specimens. He said there were some insects in Menang which are exceedingly rare."

He put the paper carefully in an envelope, and tucked it in his pocket. "Of course, I told him I would be glad to oblige. And it has caused me to somewhat change my plans. I had made up my mind to leave Mrs. Kanaka at last. The pig gets larger every day, and its affection gets more and more embarrassing. But now that I may make some small contribution to scientific learning I think I shall do better

to stay. I do not think I could get as good a place as Mrs.
Kanaka's where the spiders and beetles exist in so many varieties."

The jukeboxes did fine, too, and so did the pin ball machines and the loudspeakers. We got a new bunch of them
from the States and they didn't last five minutes. When
you went into town now you couldn't go a block without
hearing a jukebox playing or see the lights on a pin ball machine flashing.

The graduates kept starting new businesses. One of them
had seen a picture in a magazine of a restaurant in Los An-
geles that was a big tea pot, with steam coming out of the
spout and had seats and tables inside. And he put up one
like it quick, and it was sure a big hit. And another seen the
picture of a orange juice place made of a big orange. And he
built a big orange where you could sit in it and drink orange
juice and orange pop the same way.

And they put up the places fast, too. Before, they'd make
the buildings of stone and it'd take them a couple of years.
Now they'd make them of plaster and boards, and they'd
put them up in a couple of weeks. Course they weren't as
big as the ones at home, but they were real pretty. And
sometimes when you'd be walking along and seeing the big
tea kettle and the big orange, and hearing the jukeboxes
play, for a minute you could think you were back in the
States.

The other students kept doing fine, too. Gunga Das was
going around with his friends on street corners, almost telling people right out they ought to get rid of the Tunku and
his brother and put in a new Tunku. And Teddy was doing
the same. And he was always taking new societies into the
Celestial Tigers. I tried to slow them down again because I
knew something was going to happen. But I couldn't do
any good any more.

"You've created a bloody Frankenstein with your school,

Oral," says Alf, when I stopped in for a beer. "You got 'em started now and I don't see any way of making 'em stop. Looks to me you've started a fire that's going to burn up this whole island. And nobody's got a bloody extinguisher. . . . Bertie, what do you want me to do with this bloody Aussie sailor says he wants a cocktail made of the medicine they use for dipping sheep? I can't find no sheep dip in stock."

It was getting time for the end of the classes again, and this was the fifth graduation. And five was a lucky number for the Chinese and the other people in Menang, and I figured we'd make it a big one. Like G.B. said, I kept trying to think of new things all the time. And the beauty contest had been such a success it'd be fine if we could think of something else just as good.

I was sitting with Mr. Bascom one afternoon, looking over some magazines, thinking maybe we'd find some ideas. And we came on a picture of a carnival they had somewhere, and that made me think right away of Mr. Bascom and the Mardi Gras in New Orleans.

"Why don't we have a kind of celebration something like a Mardi Gras for the graduation?" I said. "These people are crazy about parades and dressing up and things. The Chinese New Year's coming soon and that's the lucky day of the year. We can celebrate New Year's with a big parade and then the graduation."

Mr. Bascom gets so excited he don't even notice a big cockroach passing by. "A wonderful idea, Mr. Oral," he says. "We can have a grand ball the night before, and Miss Rani, the beauty queen of Menang, can be the queen, as my sister was of the Mardi Gras in 1913."

Well, the more we talked about it, the more excited we got. The school had been there a good while now, and we had plenty of graduates. So I figured we'd make it what they call a Old Home Week, like they have in the States, when everybody comes back. And Mr. Bascom said we ought to have caps and gowns for the graduates; we'd never done that before. And I thought that was a good idea, too, and we stayed till long after supper talking.

Next day I talked to the students and the people who'd been at the school, and some of the people in town, besides. And the more I talked about it, the bigger and better it got. I figured we'd have a parade with floats, with each graduate of the school that had a store or something making a little float advertising what he was doing. And everybody said it was fine. Course I figured we'd have the best float of all for the school, a pasteboard boat with a big sign, *Menang Success School*. And in the middle'd be a big gold throne, with Rani sitting on it wearing her golden crown and a ribbon across her "Miss Menang."

With a big parade like that we had to have a lion dance the way they always do there. So the men began cutting up big cloth lion skins; one man becomes the lion's head and the other is his tail. And the men and the women that sang the operas began fixing new costumes for the grand ball. And the ones to graduate began making their caps and gowns from the magazine pictures I gave them; only they made them red instead of black, because black like blue was one of the colors of mourning.

There were sixty-five graduating this time and I tell you the boat was sure humming with everybody cutting and sewing. And plenty of places in town where you went you'd see the people getting the floats ready, plastering and hammering and sawing.

I was in my room late one night, when I hear Teddy hurrying up the plank, and when he comes that time of day I know he ain't feeling good.

"O Tuan, I have just heard," he says. "The priests and the mullahs have been meeting today with the Tunku's brother. They say the beauty contest between the young girls has shamed the gods so much even the volcano is in mourning and has covered her face with ashes. And now they say all these new things you plan will shame the gods further. They say such shame and the other things you have done with the school can be borne no longer. Very soon when the stars are right they will come again to destroy the boat. And this time they say they will not fail."

Well, we'd heard that before, and we were still there, so I wasn't too much worried. And we went on thinking up plans for the graduation.

One thing bothered me was making the speech when you give the graduates diplomas. G.B. was wonderful doing it, but speech-making sure ain't for me. And there wasn't anything I'd read in the comic books about people graduating from college. Only thing about colleges was a young fellow studying to be a scientist that got mad at one of the professors that insulted him and went off to Mars and persuaded the Mars people to attack the earth, and they wiped out the college with a death ray. And I seen a couple of college movies where young fellows were working their way through playing saxophones and electric guitars, and had their rooms full of footballs and girls. But they didn't help much on a speech.

But after looking a while Mr. Bascom found a book that he'd had, told all about graduating. And he helped me and pretty soon I had a speech, about how graduating was like setting out in a ship over a stormy sea where you'd never been before, but when you had something like the school at your side, you knew in the end you'd get through safe to your port. And I began practicing it while Mu Lan and Mock Duck and Amok and Teddy listened. And they all said it sounded fine.

Well, the day before New Year's came, when the Chinese make a big fuss over the Kitchen God; they believe that on New Year's day the god goes off to Heaven to make his report on the people where he's been living. And Mock Duck gave him peanut candy and fresh betel nut, and everything else you could think of. And he put so much of my whisky on the god's lips if the god could have drunk it he'd have sure fell down.

And he gave the cat some special fish because he said that at New Year's if the cat wanted to he could pray for his master's prosperity. And a praying cat, like a praying tiger, was something they liked to see in Heaven.

"The cat is an object of special reverence throughout most of these tropical islands," said Mr. Bascom. "I have made a slight study of the subject since my coming. I have heard that on certain holy days the natives tie a small prayer to a cat's tail, and each time the tail wags the prayer is said by the cat, similar to the turning of the prayer wheel."

We put the finishing touches on the room for the big ball to be held that night. And it looked wonderful all fixed up with hundreds of orchids and red and white flowers and Menang and American flags. The people started coming at six o'clock, though the party didn't start till eight. Most of them didn't have watches so they ain't so good about time. Mu Lan and all the other girls had beautiful new dresses; even the poorest person in Menang had to have a new suit or dress for New Year's or something terrible'd happen.

And then the people that sung in the operas arrive dressed like gypsies and Egyptian soldiers, and bullfighters and clowns. And then Rani comes in wearing a beautiful dress this time white silk all covered with white things like fishscales that shine like pieces of looking glass. And her hair's fixed up like in the movies; she looks just like the picture of Miss America on the wall. And everybody claps and of course she's the queen of them all.

She gives me a lovely smile. "This is the dress I bought

with the money when I sold the sewing machine, Tuan,"
she says. "So it is really a present from you."

And then it's eight o'clock and Mr. Bascom comes out
and stands in front of the orchestra. He had got himself up
in a evening suit and it must have been a hundred years
old—I guess he'd had it put away somewhere so the beetles
hadn't been able to eat it. He looks like a picture of Stone-
wall Jackson my grandfather had on his wall back home. I
move beside Rani, and take her arm, and everybody lines up
behind us. And Mr. Bascom taps the little stick he's holding and everybody gets quiet. And the orchestra begins to
play, and Rani and me start walking down the hall in what
they call the Grand March. And I tell you it was the proud-
est minute of my life.

Well, they all start dancing then, and course dancing ain't
for me. So I let Rani go and she starts dancing with a rich
Chinese fellow is the biggest rice merchant in town.

And after that she's dancing with somebody every minute. The Frenchman that owned the big rubber plantation
was there, too. I didn't want him to come at first, but she
kept on asking, and her face started to get like the mask; and
then I said yes, and so he came, looking like Rockefeller's
brother. But she only dances a couple of dances with him,
and each time she's finished she looks at me and smiles
awful sweet, and of course I feel fine.

The music changes then and Mr. Bascom comes away
from the orchestra. And he takes Rani by the arm, and they
start a dance he'd taught her and the other girls, a dance
they call the polka. And to see him going around the floor
was like you were visiting New Orleans and the wax figures
had come to life in the old governor's palace that's a museum. And then they stop, and Mr. Bascom, all out of
breath, gives Rani to somebody else.

"The polka is a beautiful dance," he tells me. "In my

estimation second only to the waltz. It is a Polish dance, as you know. I find the dances of the Poles most attractive, though their politics, I am informed, are quite obnoxious."

Well, everybody danced and danced, doing waltzes and polkas and grand right and left, and sometimes swing dances and the twist. And then twelve o'clock struck, and it was New Year's, and we began shooting off firecrackers. And we'd got the biggest strings of them in Menang, and it sounded like the time I was in the army down at Fort Polk, when a soldier lit a cigarette and the whole ammunition depot blew up.

The people started dancing again, and they danced until two. And then the orchestra played *Good Night, Ladies* the way Mr. Bascom had taught them, and everybody went home. Rani comes up with her mother and pressed my hands, the way she always did, and I could see she'd had a wonderful time. And everybody on the way out said it was the finest party that'd ever been in Menang.

Well, I didn't get much sleep because at daybreak the firecrackers started going off all over town, loud enough to wake everybody in a graveyard. But after a wonderful night like that, and with the parade and the graduation coming next, I sure wouldn't have slept anyway.

The crowd started coming even before breakfast, like they did for the beauty contest, and pretty soon it was the biggest ever. They weren't just from the city this time; they came from all over the island. They were packed thick as ants around a spilled sack of sugar. And every once in a while somebody'd shoot off a string of firecrackers, and everybody'd jump and laugh, and it was really exciting.

And then Mr. Bascom came and he was looking happy. "The New Year starts out excellently," he said. "I had a neighbor, an Italian gentleman, who stayed in the adjoining house. As you know a sewing machine is very costly here and very attractive to the women. This Italian had bought a fine machine and he rented it to his female friends, but the rent—" he cleared his throat "—was very high, and his parties were very disturbing. This morning I learned he is moving with the machine and its users to another part of the city."

The floats started coming a little while later and they were sure pretty, some of them on trucks and some of them pulled by oxen and buffalo. And Mr. Bascom and I began lining them up for the parade. First came the lions, with a Chinese fellow holding a big whip, like he was the trainer. And they did the lion dance and all kinds of tricks that had the people holding their sides to keep their clothes from busting. And right behind the trainer and the lions came the band. And the band'd been hired for a wedding a week or so back, and they'd learned the *Wedding March*, so they were playing that now.

After the band came the first float, fixed up by the fellow had the new restaurant in the tea kettle, just like they'd have back home; it was a big plaster tea kettle with steam coming out the spout and people sitting inside at a table drinking tea. And after that was a big plaster orange made by the fellow owned the new orange juice place, with people inside drinking orange pop out of bottles with straws.

Gunga Das had a fine float, a real American barber shop with a barber pole and a man in a chair getting shaved; and Tak Thong had a float with a big Sleeping Buddha and some monks sitting beside it, and it was pulled by two sacred cows. And each of them had a sign saying "Graduate Menang Success School," and that was nice for us, and for Menang, too. There were a bunch of others, but I guess these were the best. The lady that ran the loveboat wanted to have a float, too, but we figured it wouldn't be so nice.

At the end was the float of the school like I'd planned, the model of the boat with the gold throne for Rani, showing she was the queen of the school as well as Menang. And around the throne a dozen of the graduates were sitting, all fixed up with red caps and gowns.

There still wasn't any sign of Rani, but I knew how she always came just at the last minute. And I knew how she'd gone to bed awful late, so I didn't get worried.

Well, fifteen minutes passed, and then a half hour, and it was getting close to starting time. And she still hadn't come and then I did begin to get nervous.

"Has anybody seen Rani?" I said to the students on the school truck. But none of them knew anything.

Another fifteen minutes passed, and now it was really time to go, and everybody got in line. And the drivers of the trucks climbed up on the seats and the drivers of the ox and buffalo carts took hold of the bridles; and the band started playing the *Wedding March*, and they all got ready to move off. But still there wasn't a sign of her.

"Maybe she's sick," I said to one of the Hindu girls that knew her best. "I thought last night a couple of times she looked kind of nervous and tired."

Rani lived just a block or so away now, because they'd got a better place since she won the contest. And I asked the Hindu girl to go over to her house and see what was the matter.

Another ten minutes passed, and the girl hadn't come back, and the people in the parade was getting restless. I was just going to send another girl to find out what's happened, when I see the first one come running down the street, all excited. Somebody's with her, but it isn't Rani, and when they come close I see it's her mother. And the mother's crying and carrying on something awful. And behind her are a bunch of Hindu women, and they're crying and carrying on, too.

And something terrible hits me, and I say to the mother, "Is . . . is . . . she dead?"

And the mother shakes her head, but I don't know

whether she means yes or no, and she starts crying and carrying on worse, and talks something wild in Hindu.

I'm going kind of crazy now. "What is it?" I ask the Hindu girl. "What's she saying?"

She kind of hesitates. "O Tuan, it is terrible," she answers. "Rani has run off with the rich Frenchman that owns the rubber plantation. He told her he would take her to Paris. To be married, he said. She flew off with him to Jakarta this morning. In the beautiful dress she was wearing last night at the ball, Tuan."

Chapter XV

I felt like I never felt in my life before. It was like . . . like one time I was diving in the water hole in the creek back of Muleshoe that was always twenty feet deep, and this time I dived and everything went kind of like big streaks of lightning flashing inside me, because I'd hit my head on some rocks. And when I came to I was laying in the hospital where they'd operated on me to save my life.

And then everything was kind of a blur for a minute, and then the blur faded and I felt somebody by me, holding my hand, and I saw it was Mu Lan. And then I saw Rani's mother and the other Hindu women crying and carrying on, and I knew I wasn't in the hospital, and there wasn't any operation would help me. I was in Menang and Rani was gone. And then I saw the people on the floats waiting and heard the band playing, and I knew I'd have to go on some way.

How I did it, I'll never know. I guess you heard of people having a leg shot off in a war, and then feeling pain in it and even walking on it a little way. I guess it's the same kind of thing maybe. And I saw the throne on the school float all empty, and somebody, maybe Mr. Bascom or maybe me, asked Mu Lan to sit in it, and she did, and the parade started.

The parade went all around town as if nothing had happened, and then broke up near the wharf. And then all the old students from the floats and the new ones that were getting diplomas came into the big room on the boat, and began getting ready for the graduation.

The room was packed with the families of the graduates, but there were a few rows of seats at the back for the people from Menang. And a big crowd of them were standing on the deck outside, watching through the doors and windows.

Teddy's yellow head was getting like the pancakes again, when the dough is still kind of raw. I could see he was getting awful nervous.

"There is something queer going on, Tuan," he says. "There are men here with faces I do not like. The nose of a man who has been poor becomes like that of a rabbit who can smell a fox; he can smell trouble the same way. My nose is quivering with the trouble smells now, Tuan."

And a couple of minutes later I see him and Gunga Das move outside and go down the gangplank.

I take my seat up on the platform with the graduates, looking like temple monks in their red caps and gowns. And then everybody stops talking and Mr. Bascom touches me awful gentle.

"It is time to make the speech, Mr. Oral," he says.

And I make it though I guess I must have sounded like I was talking some new, crazy kind of language; because I don't think the words I said could have made sense. And then some of the graduates come up, the seventy-year-old fellow that got married, and the little fellow who swept up that's the boxer, and some of the warehouse clerks that have got shops now. And they make little speeches and say how they owe everything to the school. And then the students come up one by one in their red caps and gowns, and I start handing out the diplomas.

Suddenly there's a shot outside, and at first I think it's a loud firecracker. But it must have been some kind of signal. Because I see people jumping up from the back seats, and a lot of others come busting in from outside, and a second later half a dozen men are on me. I fight like a tiger, but they get me down and hold me. And I look and see they've got Mu Lan and Mock Duck and Amok and Mr. Bascom the same way. Amok had put up a terrible fight, I could tell by the faces of the fellows near him. They look like they'd been kicked by a horse wearing spikes on his shoes.

Some of the students had been battling hard, too, but they never had a chance. The fellows guarding us make everybody leave, and they take Mu Lan and Mock Duck and Amok and Mr. Bascom away. And then they take me on deck and I see the fat priest of the snake temple and the other old Bomos and mullahs; he's bossing things right and left and telling everybody what to do. And Fu Manchu and the Harmonious Daggers are standing by, waiting to do anything that's needed.

The fat priest glances around and calls to some tough looking Chinese at the railing got faces like Chicago gangsters.

"Get the oil," he says.

And the tough fellows bring cans of gasoline from somewhere and start spilling it all around the doors.

The old priest walks over to see if they've done a good job. And then they take me onto the wharf. And when everybody's come down the gangplank, the priest passes out some torches and matches.

"Burn the boat," he says. And he lights a torch and is just about to throw it, when a bunch of police come running and shout to him to stop, and behind them I see the Tunku's brother.

He's dressed the same way I saw him at the Happy World, in fancy European clothes with the gold sarong like one of them burlesque queens around his waist, only this time he's got a little red hat, makes him look like a turkey gobbler. He's fatter and puffier than ever, and his eyes are like a fox just ate a couple of ducks. He reminded me more than ever of the fellow had the lunch stand in Muleshoe when he was giving you change and was getting rid of a bad quarter. And the same two fellows are with him, with their sarongs of green silk, and they've got the little turkey gobbler hats, just the same as him. They look like the Shriners' parade I seen one time when I come in from laying track when I was working out of Chattanooga.

The Tunku's brother sees me and talks to the priests; and the police take me from the tough-looking fellows and put the handcuffs on me.

"You're under arrest," says the man with the green sarong, and his voice is like acid burning you.

I ask him what for, and his voice gets even nastier.

"For inciting and teaching seditious acts against the lawful government," he says. "The penalty is hanging."

And then the Tunku's brother talks to the priests and laughs, and they start laughing, too. And I can see whatever he's saying they think it's pretty funny. And the tough fellows mop up the oil and throw away the torches.

The man in the green sarong turns to me again. "The Tunku says they will not burn your boat," he tells me. "He will make it into his private stable. Your classroom will become his stalls. Your new students will be his donkeys."

Pretty soon the police ride me off to a gloomy jail, and a big Chinese leads me through a couple of iron doors, and dumps me into a cell with a little square hole up at the top with bars across for a window. It's got a dirt floor and dirt walls full of cracks as wide as a couple of fingers. And you know that the cracks are full of all kinds of spiders and scorpions and maybe other things worse.

The big Chinese was a kind of queer fellow, laughing to himself all the time. And at first he won't answer a single question; he don't even seem to hear me. But I give him a big bill and it kind of loosens him up, and he talks just like the Chinamen they have in the Fu Manchu comics.

"What they going to do with me?" I say.

He gives a big laugh that kind of shakes down the loose dirt in the ceiling. "Two, thlee, days you stick jail. Then man bling rope and you make noise like chicken. Ho! Ho!" And he puts his hand at his neck as if he's being hung, and gives a squawk like a hen that's having her eggs taken from under her, and laughs till he's double pretty near.

"What about the other people?" I ask, meaning Mu Lan and the rest.

"All same thing, like chicken. Ho! Ho!"

There ain't any chair in the cell, just a couple of sacks of straw instead of a bed. I sit down on a sack, and try to think. And for a while all I can think of is Rani, and the awful thing she did. And then I think of Mu Lan and how fine she is, and try to think of some way of getting out so I can help her. I put the two sacks on top of each other, and that way can reach the bars over the little window. And I try to shake them loose till I'm blue in the face, but they're as solid as rock. And it gets dark and I hear the Chinaman coming, and he brings in some rice and a smoky lantern. And I try giving him more money to let me out; but he just puts his hand to his neck and squawks like a chicken again.

He come a couple of times more that night. I guess he was

getting suspicious. And each time he puts his head through the door, and gives a chicken squawk bigger than ever. He made me remember a fellow I knew at Muleshoe went to a Kiwanis convention in Chicago once and heard a joke about a traveling salesman and three old maids, and kept telling it over till he was eighty. It was the only joke he knowed.

I was awake the whole night thinking, I guess. But I couldn't think of anything. There wasn't no United States consul at Menang. They'd had one long time ago, but there'd been some kind of argument, and they never brought him back. The nearest Americans were at Jakarta, and that was hundreds of miles away.

I got up on the sacks and shook the bars again, but all I did was shake down some dust. And I tried to think of all the things I seen in the comics and the picture shows people did to get out of prison; it seemed so easy then but here none of the tricks would work.

And then I could tell the sun had come up and all day I sat on the sacks trying to figure out what I could do. And sometimes I paced up and down the dirt floor, like a tiger in a zoo. And then when it got dark the Chinaman come in with the rice and the lantern again.

"Give money," he says.

And I give him the rest of what I've got.

He puts the money in his pocket, and I think for a minute he's going to give me the key to the cell. But instead he puts his hands about his head, and motions like somebody pulling on a rope. And then he puts his hands to his throat again, and starts squawking till I thought he'd bust. And then all of a sudden he stops.

"Like chicken. Tomollow," he says, and goes out the door.

Well, I sit there by the rice and the lantern, thinking again. And I think of all the things I done in my life, the good things and the bad things, too. I think of the girls I knew in the cotton mill and when I was railroading, and especially Mu Lan and Rani. And I think about home, and the way I had to quit school, and how maybe if I'd have got a good education everything would have been different. And I wondered if the people at Muleshoe would ever find out I was dead. And then I think of Mu Lan and Mock Duck and Amok again, and Mr. Bascom, too. And I hope what's going to happen to me don't happen to them, because it's all my fault.

I guess I'm kind of dozing when I hear shots fired in the distance somewhere. And I figure maybe they've changed their minds about hanging, and are shooting everybody instead. And then in a couple of minutes I hear people running down the corridor, and I know they are coming for me. And I get ready to fight, and make them pay for what they've done, even though I know I haven't got a chance.

I hear the lock turn and I back against the wall. And then the door busts open, and I can't believe my eyes. Instead of the big Chinaman it's Teddy and Gunga Das. And Teddy throws his skinny arms around me like I was his brother, and Gunga Das stands there all smiles.

"The people have risen, Tuan," Teddy says. "The Tunku is overthrown."

And then he tells me how Gunga Das's friends and the Celestial Tigers and all the people in favor of the school had drove out the Tunku and his brother; and those two had run off in a boat, nobody knew where, and the people had put in a new Tunku that was a fine fellow, and Teddy and Gunga Das were his right hand men.

I go outside with them, pretty shaky, and I see the big black automobile that had belonged to the Harmonious Daggers. And now Mu Lan and Mock Duck and Amok and Mr. Bascom are sitting in it, and I climb in, too. And I take Mu Lan's hand and it's like when I took a chalk eraser at the blackboard when I was in school at Muleshoe; it kind of rubbed out all the bad things about Rani that'd been there in my head before.

We go back to the boat and it's still all right; they hadn't started putting in the donkeys. And I get cleaned up good after that terrible jail, and Mu Lan and all the rest of them sit talking till the sun comes up pretty near.

"I found my stay in the jail of great interest," said Mr. Bascom. "There were numerous varieties of beetles and I collected one or two specimens which I think may be quite rare. And my human companions who shared my cell were equally worthy of study. They were five in number, one a Chinese graduate of the school, though I had not known him before. He taught me a card game, quite Oriental, called fan-tan, which we all found full of fascination. He won all the money I and the others had, but he was very generous. He allowed us to give IOU's."

They all go home and I go to sleep, and I don't wake up till noon. And I'm getting ready to have breakfast when I hear a roaring outside, and I see a big crowd on the wharf. And I grab my gun and load it up, thinking they're coming to attack the boat again. And then I hear a band playing off in the distance and I put the gun away. I see the people ain't mad at all, they're all smiling and happy.

The band comes around the corner to the boat, and they're playing the *Wedding March* again; they ain't had time to learn anything new. And in back of them is the new Tunku in a automobile big as a hearse. On one side of him a servant is sitting, holding a gold umbrella over his head. And on the other side is a nice-looking boy, maybe sixteen, that I can tell right off is the Tunku's son. And in the back seat, sitting pretty as catbirds, are Teddy and Gunga Das.

They all walk slow up the gangplank with the servant still holding the umbrella. And the Tunku starts talking to me, but I don't understand the language.

"He says he has come to put his son in your school,

Tuan," Teddy tells me. "He says he wishes to show his appreciation of what the school did for Menang."

And I guess that was coming pretty far for a boy from Muleshoe, Kentucky.

And then a lot of the crowd on the wharf come onto the boat wanting to join the school, the same way. And there were so many and they came so fast we ran out of paper and pens getting their names.

I guess it was a few weeks after that I started the American history class again. And it was full this time, because the new Tunku's son was there. The new Tunku said he wanted his boy to know something about a country that made people like G.B. and me. Mu Lan was there, too, like she'd always been, even though she'd had the class two or three times now. The class that day is America in the early days again, and I'm telling them about the Indians and Captain John Smith and Pocahontas, when all of a sudden a queer thing happens never happened to me before.

Like I said it's queer how it is with your brain; how things in your mind run all together like the numbers in a Bingo machine and then come out any which way.

I'm standing there telling what a wonderful person Pocahontas was, saving Captain John Smith from the Indians. And I happen to look at Mu Lan and like a lightning flash she ain't Mu Lan any more; she's turned into Pocahontas. The more I look and the more I think about it the more the two of them are the same. Whenever I needed somebody, like with the kuntaow or the acapuncture or when any kind of trouble came along, Mu Lan was always right there by my side, waiting to stroke the pain away or give her life for me if she had to.

I felt so kind of queer I could hardly get through the lesson.

The feeling was so strong if I believed in that what they call reincarnation, like Rani done, I'd have been sure that

Mu Lan was Pocahontas way back, and I was Captain John Smith, the Englishman.

I know it was all crazy. I can't figure what made my brain go around that way. Maybe because I read once in a comic about the Indians that the Indians come from the Chinese. It was a good comic, that Indian one. I'm sorry they ain't got it any more.

That night after supper it was kind of hot and I took Mu Lan out to the Happy World to cool off. We were by ourselves this time because after that day on the volcano her sister didn't always come along. Like I said, they'd fixed up the park all fancy, like Coney Island, and you could hear our jukeboxes playing and the pin ball machines ringing everywhere.

But they still had the elephant, and we took a ride on him like we done when I first come to Menang.

And then a funny thing. All of a sudden it happened again; the girl I was riding with wasn't Mu Lan—it was Pocahontas, all in Indian dress and feathers.

I seen her plain as day, coming up and cutting the ropes the Indians had tied me with, so I could escape, and then getting down on her knees and asking her father Powhatan to pardon her and me.

And then there come another kind of lightning flash and I knew now it was Mu Lan, not Rani, I'd really loved all the time, the way Captain John Smith loved Pocahontas.

The elephant got to the end of his walk and stopped by the high platform there, waiting for us to get off. But neither of us moved. I was kind of stunned, I guess. And I guess Mu Lan seen how I was and didn't want to upset me. And the fellow that drove the elephant figured we wanted another ride. So he started the elephant off again.

And then we finally came back to the platform and I helped her down. And like before it was like you was touching a feather.

We walked along slow, kind of hand in hand.

"Maybe you ain't exactly Pocahontas," I said to her. "But you're the same to me as she was to Captain John Smith. And I know you'd have sure saved my life plenty of times if there'd ever been any bad Indians around."

For a minute she looked kind of mixed up, like she didn't understand. And then her face got the way it did when we were at the Happy World the first time and she came through the gate and seen all the lights and everything. It was like the face of the lady on the Sunday School cards when she dies and becomes a saint and finds out she's going to heaven.

Well, not long after there was a lot of people come all dressed up to the house of Mu Lan's rich uncle for another wedding. And the courts like the Chinese boxes were full of kids and everybody shooting off firecrackers and spit-devils. And I guess you've already figured, this time the people being married were Mu Lan and me.

And Mu Lan looked as if she was a beautiful doll the Chinaman in Muleshoe had in a glass box he said was a Chinese princess. Her wedding dress was a present from her uncle and course wasn't a dress at all; it was a soft yellow jacket and trousers, made all of satin and covered all over with gold and silver embroidered flowers. The slippers were yellow satin, too, and embroidered the same way. In her hair there was a high gold comb bigger than her little head pretty near; at one side by her ear was a big yellow flower. And her face was all shining like when we rode in the dragon boat the first night at the Happy World. She sure looked like a beautiful flower herself, just the same as her name.

Course her sister and Mock Duck were there and Teddy and Amok, too. And Mr. Bascom in his evening suit looking like a wax figure again out of the museum, and Alf and Bertie, dressed to kill.

There was a lot of bowing and scraping, and then I took out a pair of fancy earrings and put them in Mu Lan's ears. And then her uncle opened up what looked like the little tombstones in the wall Mu Lan said were the tablets of her ancestors. And I took her hand and we knelt before them together. And Mu Lan introduced me to all the dead members of her family, and the uncle wrote my name in the family book, and said some day I'd have a tablet up there, too. And that way we were married.

And all the old ladies teased Mu Lan and told her, "Remember we said, 'You next'?" And she smiled and blushed and took my hand again and led me to the big table set maybe for two hundred people.

And then all the little kids said, "Grandfather, please eat rice," again. And we ate a Chinese meal I ain't got over yet. And then I took her back to the boat and we knelt before the Kitchen God, and Mu Lan introduced me to him, too. And Mock Duck told him I was sorry I forgot the betel nut that time, and please not to hold it against me, and made me give him a whole bottle of whisky.

Mu Lan's sure been a wonderful wife, and we have a wonderful life together. And queer thing, every once in a while, she looks like Pocahontas again.

We stayed in Menang a couple of years more and everything was fine. We had so many people asking to come to the school we could have used three boats if we'd have wanted. And the jukeboxes and the pin ball machines went so fast we had to bring them from the States pretty near by the boatload. And there wasn't a temple now didn't have a loudspeaker outside the gate; so there wasn't a place in town where you couldn't hear the temple bells tinkle.

Instead of all the little rug shops making rugs by hand, there was was one big rug factory started by a fellow from the school with 300 people working for him. They'd all sit in a line working like lightning, just like they do in the auto plants the way I seen in the pictures. And instead of taking maybe a year to make a rug, they could turn one out every minute. At the Happy World they had motors in the dragon boats that got them around the little rivers fast. And there were jazz orchestras everywhere and people dancing in night clubs till four o'clock in the morning. So when the people came off the big cruise boats, there was somewhere for them to go. It was sure a wonderful place now. Like I said, when you walked around you couldn't have told that you wasn't in the States.

Only one thing, Mr. Bascom had become kind of crazy about card playing; you'd see him playing with somebody whenever he had even a minute. And every once in a while he'd lose a month or so of his salary.

"I find this fan-tan excellent stimulation for the mind," he would say. "Though I have never seen players the equal of the ones I met on that occasion in the jail. If I knew they were still there, now that I am more familiar with the game, I would like to go back for a visit."

And then Teddy came running in one night to tell me they've had a new revolution. And they'd got a new Tunku, a kind of hillbilly from back in the jungle, and Teddy and Gunga Das had to get out, and I figured things being the way they were we'd better do the same. We'd been kind of wanting a change anyway.

So we packed up fast and got in a boat and came to Singapore. We been here a couple of months, trying to figure out where we're going next, and what we're going to do. I been thinking about it and looking around and talking it over with Mu Lan and plenty of people. And since we did so fine with the Success School, I figure the best thing to do is to start one of them physical culture schools and gymnasiums that's all the rage here in Singapore.

They're like the ones run by the fellow back in the States called himself Mister Hercules. You know the fellow, all the time shows his muscles in the back of the comics and what they call the Mister magazines. He's got a couple of places here in Singapore and they're going day and night. And course for me there ain't nothing makes me happy like doing something educational.

Gymnasium is pretty near the last word in the G's in the dictionary. The first word in the G's is gab, that's kind of slang for talk.

I been looking over the map trying to figure out where to go. And we couldn't decide until the other day when I was walking along the docks and I seen somebody looked familiar. And what do you know, it turns out it was my old buddy G.B. He'd been off in the South Sea islands, he said, selling machines to make ice cream cones. He was doing fine, because people out there sure like things sweet and cold. Until the fellows he sold them to found out the machines were so old it wasn't even the same kind of electricity they're using today.

Course it wasn't G.B.'s fault. He bought them when they were cleaning out a big warehouse in Hong Kong. And G.B. says they made him pay a terrible price and swore to him they were the latest kind of cone machines there is. They sure cheated him all right.

The natives didn't cut him up too bad, he said. He was only in the hospital two months.

I was sure glad to see him, because I'd missed him plenty, ever since the day he'd been gone. He said he'd like to start the physical culture school and the gymnasium, and he said he'd go with us right away.

"I figure we'll go to Bali," he says. "That's a beautiful place, full of beautiful girls, and they ain't ever had a school like that on the island. I figure we ought to do fine. They're all little fellows there and all little fellows want to be big."

We'll be going in a couple of weeks, soon as we sell some things we brought from Menang, and I lend G.B. the money to pay some people to get him out of trouble some crook got him into here in Singapore again. Like I said, I'm sure glad I found him again. He's sure a wonderful fellow.

I was talking with a fellow came in a boat from Menang, just yesterday, and I got a shock. He said the new Tunku's changed everything back the way it used to be before we came with the school. He said the monks in the temples have gone back to all the old ways. They've got the big hats again so they can't see how much the people are putting in the begging bowls, and they're taking six months again to carve the little Buddhas. And they've torn down the rug factory with the people working in a line and they just sit around and work and talk the way they used to do before. And the Happy World was like it was the first time I went there with Mu Lan, with the little dragon boats you rowed on the little rivers, past the willow trees and the red bridges and the little red pagodas. And in town the big tea kettle and orange were gone.

None of the people were dancing the twist; they were doing the old-time Malay dances. Only thing left from the school was the waltz, and Mr. Bascom was still teaching them that. There wasn't a single jazz orchestra, only them queer kind of Malay orchestras playing gongs. And they'd broke up every loudspeaker and jukebox on the island. I can't figure out why they'd do it.

People sure are funny.

About the Author

Ben Lucien Burman, who was born in the river town of Covington, Kentucky, has been called America's greatest living interpreter. He is famous for his novels of the Mississippi. His *Steamboat Round the Bend,* which became Will Rogers's most successful film, and *Blow for a Landing* have become American classics.

Mr. Burman wrote his first story on a toy typewriter when he was seven years old and has been writing ever since. He was wounded during World War I at Soissons, and his writing was interrupted for a while, but after the war he became a reporter for the Boston *Herald,* and later for the old New York *World.* When Burman was twenty-six he gave up newspaper work to concentrate on fiction.

The author, with his wife, Alice Caddy, who illustrates

his books, has traveled widely in the Far East and in Southeast Asia, where they collected material for *The Sign of the Praying Tiger.*

Mr. Burman's books have been translated into many languages and he has been decorated by the French government with the Legion of Honor. He is frequently referred to as the modern Mark Twain.